MAX'S CAMPERVAN CASE FILES BOOK 10

ISLAND OF Death

TYLER RHODES

Copyright © 2024 Tyler Rhodes

All rights reserved. This book or any portion thereof may not be reproduced or used in any manner whatsoever without the express written permission of the author except for the use of brief quotations in a book review.

This is a work of fiction. Names, characters, businesses, places, events and incidents are either the products of the author's imagination or used in a fictitious manner. Any resemblance to actual persons, living or dead, or actual events is purely coincidental.

Dedicated to all the wonderful folk of Cornwall. You lucky things.

Chapter 1

"Can't you row any faster?" I teased, craning my neck then straining hard with the oars as they sliced through the perfectly calm water of the English Channel.

Anxious, my best buddy and the most adorable Jack Russell Terrier in Cornwall, glanced up from where he'd been leaning over the side and "helping" by splashing with a tiny paw, causing the rowing boat to wobble. Eyes wide with concern, he whined then hurriedly centred himself on the small bench seat at the stern and barked his answer.

"I understand, and yes, it is quite scary. You're doing great, and are super brave."

Another bark, then he sat up straight, cocked his head to the side, and studied me intently as he always did when he either wasn't quite sure about something, or was frustrated.

"Not long now. We'll be at the island in about ten minutes. The guy we hired the boat from said it's an easy row, and all we have to do is stay within the marker buoys and we'll be fine. No need to worry."

We both turned to study the small island that sat proudly half a mile off the Cornish coast, not too far from the much more impressive St Michael's Mount slightly further east, but it certainly had its own charm. The ruins of a castle stood in stark relief against a clear, beautiful blue sky, the castle dark and brooding, almost like a cardboard cut-out pinned to the island itself.

I'd been told that it wasn't as large as it seemed, and that the island was tiny, home to only a handful of residents. When I enquired exactly how many, the gruff man renting me the boat had stared at me like I was daft, then repeated that a handful of people lived there.

"You mean five?" I asked.

With his eyes locked on mine, he smiled sadly, shook his head and adjusted his greasy fisherman's cap, then counted out the fingers on one hand slowly. He glared at me to make sure his point hit home, then smoothed down his blue smock that stank of fish as if it would calm his nerves. "Yes, five," he hissed, then took my money, explained about the boat, helped us in, and shoved us out into the water. I'd wanted to get more information about the residents, and what exactly went on at the island beyond it being an oddity sitting low and alone in the sea, but John had other ideas and seemingly just wanted us gone.

Now here we were, a man and his dog, rocking in the water, still trying to figure out how to beat the tide that wanted to take us back to shore rather than to the mysterious island I was doing my best to approach.

The sun beat down and I had to hold back any complaints, as this was why we'd hurried to Cornwall after our previous adventure a few weeks ago. Now at the bitter end of September, most of the country was enveloped in cloud and rain, but here in the south the climate was unseasonably warm, and I rejoiced at once more being back in cut-offs, a black vest, and my trusty, but now very well-worn, Crocs. Oh, how I loved my unstylish, but beyond comfortable footwear. I refused to wear anything else as long as the weather held up, and so far we'd had two glorious weeks in Cornwall where the sun was kind and the people even kinder.

Nobody had died, nothing mysterious had happened, and Anxious and I had enjoyed ourselves immensely travelling around several stunning locations. We even spent some time in Newquay where I almost learned to surf—

Anxious got the hang of it within hours, much to my chagrin.

After a day to recover, we'd visited St Michael's Mount and walked across the causeway at low tide then back again as the waves lapped at my ankles and Anxious' tummy, and even had a few days in Penzance and Mousehole before coming back up the coast and settling at an amazing camping spot. Here we'd remained for the past week. Relaxing walks on the beach, one-pot wonders every single night, sightseeing, and plenty of just sitting outside Vee, my incredible 1967 VW Campervan, had been a true delight. I felt recharged, relaxed, and ready for an adventure today.

My best friend felt the same way, and his eyes glinted with excitement as he studied the island while seagulls swept low, checking if we had any food then heading to shore to bother the tourists still out in surprising force at the end of the season.

"Hey, Anxious, I've got a surprise for you," I teased, heaving on the oars, pleased to see we were actually making progress and should arrive in a few minutes.

With a high-pitched woof of inquiry, he ducked under my seat then leapt into my lap, causing me to almost lose hold of the oars. I suddenly felt very aware of where we were and how disastrous it would be if we became stranded out here, but couldn't help laughing as he sat up and stared into my eyes with his brown orbs of utter trust and love.

"Be careful! We could have lost the oars or you could have fallen in. I know the man gave you a little lifejacket and I have mine, but we don't want to be bobbing about in the water for hours waiting to be rescued." I pulled the oars in so they rested on the floor of the boat then swept my hair back from my face. The wind had other ideas, and my now rather wild brown locks blew straight back into my face, but it felt like freedom to me. A sharp staccato laugh escaped my salty lips and my spirits remained high.

"Fine, I'll tell you," I laughed as Anxious pawed at my bare knees. "Min's coming!"

The poor thing searched in all directions, then whined when he came up short, so I hurriedly explained. "She's going to meet us back on the mainland in a few hours. She's been mad busy with work, and we haven't seen her for weeks, so when I spoke to her yesterday she asked if it would be alright to come. I said yes, of course, and apparently she's on her way. Min got the train, so won't be long. She's going to stay all weekend. Won't that be great?"

I waited for an answer, then realised I might have overwhelmed the little guy with too much information, so said, "We'll see Min later," which seemed to satisfy him. He jumped down, padded across the boat, then resumed his seat to "help" navigate as I re-aligned the oars and rowed, ignoring the tightness in my back and my burning muscles as we slowly battled the tide and approached the island.

The one thing I'd always found odd about rowing was that you were facing away from where you were headed. It meant I had to turn constantly to check, as Anxious' directions were less than accurate. If I'd left it to him, we'd have missed the island by a mile and been munching on baguettes in France rather than pasties in Cornwall.

Nevertheless, we made good progress and soon I spied a small jetty where several other rowing boats were moored along with a speedboat I assumed one of the residents must own, or possibly it was a communal vessel so the islanders could get to the mainland for provisions. I wondered who lived here full-time and what such a life would be like. Were there children? What about school? What if the weather was bad? How did they heat their homes? Did they even have electricity? How could they? So many questions, and I looked forward to finding out the answers.

"Not long now, buddy. This will be fun. We can explore for an hour or two, then we'll head back to shore. We'll check out the castle, see what else is here, and chill out. There's a nice little beach, and the whole island only takes ten minutes to walk around apparently. Cool adventure or what?"

Anxious whined when the boat rocked, and my heart leapt into my mouth as I stressed about going overboard, but things soon settled down and after I checked over my shoulder I adjusted our position by using a single oar, then continued rowing towards the jetty. Why the man renting the boats only had four I couldn't quite fathom, but this wasn't exactly a hotbed for the tourists and the price he charged meant he must make decent money during the season.

With a bump against the rickety looking wooden jetty, I pulled the oars in, grabbed hold of a rope dangling from a massive iron ring set into the wood, then carefully secured the boat, trying, and failing, to not stress about the rocking that was making me decidedly queasy. Unlike Min, I preferred solid ground under my feet at all times, whereas she adored fairground rides and anything that had an edge —I never could understand the attraction.

Steeling myself, I cradled Anxious who snuggled down deep under my vest, whimpering slightly, then gingerly stepped onto the jetty, sighing with relief once we were on terra firma.

"Time to explore." I lowered him and he yipped for joy racing around me in circles then had a celebratory wee against the rope. "Hey, I have to touch that later. Not cool, Anxious. Not cool at all."

He grinned at me then barked for me to hurry up, so with a final check the boat was secure, I turned my attention to this small, mysterious island the tourists seemed to mostly overlook, and instantly realised why. "Um, I think we've made a terrible mistake."

My trusting companion sat and cocked his head; this was an excursion full of mystery not only for the little fella but for me too. We took a worrying moment to study what we'd let ourselves in for. Or, more to the point, the utter lack of what awaited us.

The harbour consisted of the thankfully sturdy but short jetty, the few rowing boats and speedboat, and not much else. No large harbour walls protruding into the sea, just a simple wall protecting the row of houses from the rising water. To the east I noted a rocky shore with small coves of incredibly pristine white sand. The harbour was paved with cobbles worn smooth over centuries according to the tourist information back on the mainland, built then repaired as needed ever since the castle was first constructed many centuries ago as a lookout for those living in the area but mostly as a rather eccentric folly for the rich and powerful local lord.

It seemed that was about the end of it here apart from a row of five attached cottages, each painted a different colour. Red, white, blue, pink, and green. They were clearly well-maintained, the paint so fresh it might have still been wet. I had expected to see a tourist shop, certainly a cafe and ice-cream kiosk—the usual tourist stuff—but there was nothing of the kind. What I did spy, yet almost overlooked, was a squat, ugly building covered in brown pebbledash with a sign indicating it housed the public conveniences.

My eyes trailed past the houses and up the steep bluff behind, the rear of the houses built right up against and possibly into the cliff itself. Steps were carved into the rock and meandered up to the high point where the craggy ruins of a not-so-impressive castle but in miniature sat morosely, slowly crumbling under the harsh conditions that would batter it during storms. Salt had eaten away at the mortar, eroding the facade and the once-impressive edifice that crumbled year after year, until now it was little beyond a single story with a tower pointing accusingly to the sky like a crooked finger. It leaned so much I was amazed it still stood, and doubted it was accessible which was a shame as the views would have been incredible.

Everywhere else I looked I saw nothing beyond the stripped back, bare island itself. Rock, paths, scrubby grass, and determined weeds covered most of the land, with stunted trees, bent and gnarled, growing away from the wind so they were lopsided and almost devoid of leaves.

I spied someone fishing from the low cliffs, and a few more people walking the path that made a circuit of the island.

"I need a pee," I informed Anxious, so we left the jetty and walked along the wide cobbled street that led to the houses and up to the steps then across to the sad-looking toilet block.

Anxious waited while I walked up the ramp then around the side of the building past the ladies to the gents. I grabbed the railing then frowned as my hand came away sticky. I panicked it was bird poo, but it seemed like it was jam, or possibly tomato ketchup, but how would that be here? Sniffing tentatively, I couldn't figure it out, so continued, then paused. The green door was closed, the paint peeling off the warped wood. A handprint in red about head height then smeared halfway down stopped me dead in my tracks, my fingers on the handle.

"Blood?"

Checking I was alone, I turned the handle and stepped inside, fearing the worst. The stall doors were open and empty, nobody was by the urinal, the tap at the single sink was crimson, and running, the bowl stained pink. I scooped water over the tap then rinsed my hands before turning it off, the silence total and extremely ominous. The room was claustrophobic, absolutely stank as it clearly wasn't cleaned regularly, and charged with a menacing tension, but I had to pee. I did so as fast as I could, washed up, then got out and sucked down fresh, salty air before returning to Anxious.

He sniffed the air, and whined, his ears flat to his head, so I bent and gave him a fuss before straightening and searching for anything out of place. Something wasn't right here. I knew it. I'd been involved in enough mysteries to get a sense for things, and the less-than-subtle handprint on the door and the blood on the railing made it clear something was amiss. Or was I letting my imagination get the better of me? Maybe it was just sauce. Someone might have got their hands covered in ketchup and went in to wash up, or maybe a fisherman had used the facilities after gutting fish. Yes, that was probably it.

We walked back towards the row of houses then past them, and I spied a lone building nestled into the rock, so plain I almost missed it. An unobtrusive sign declared it was called Tea Room, and with nobody else about now I figured this must be where the other tourists were, or up at the castle. A cuppa would be perfect to calm my nerves, so I set my bag down on a chair at the only table, then pushed open the door. Anxious barked then shot off into the gloomy interior, so I followed him inside. The door remained open, the bright exterior so different to the cloying dark atmosphere, and it took a moment for my eyes to adjust.

The cafe was empty.

"Hello?"

Nobody came, and now I thought about it, I couldn't smell anything. No sausages cooking, no tea brewing, not even a whiff of coffee or the noise of a machine. What was the deal here?

I returned to the door and noted the opening times. They literally opened for a few hours every afternoon and we were half an hour early. I guess they left the place unlocked as crime wouldn't be an issue here.

Chuckling to recover my nerve, I sank into a bleached green plastic chair and pulled out my phone to check on Min, but I had no signal and would have to wait until we returned to shore to call her.

"Guess we should have an explore and come back later for a cuppa," I told Anxious.

He yipped happily, keen to stretch his legs, so I grabbed my bag and decided to walk around the island before heading up to the castle. The buoyant Terrier raced off ahead towards the north where the path curved around to the right, so I smiled as I strolled leisurely after him, enjoying the wind blowing my hair out of my face, the gorgeous scent of salt and fish carried on the balmy breeze.

I turned the corner and spied a man fishing up ahead off a rocky outcropping, and figured I could ask a few questions and tell him about the handprint, but pulled up short as Anxious barked a warning then darted to the edge of the cliff and went wild yipping down into the sea.

"What are you doing? It's just the water, Anxious," I laughed, but the hairs on the back of my neck tingled and as I eased closer to the edge, I caught a smell I knew I'd never forget. I peered over and spied a large rusty anchor on the rocks below; a large chain ran from it into the water. But it wasn't the anchor that gave me pause, it was the corpse wedged awkwardly on the half ton of metal that made my head spin. I slumped to my knees and rubbed my eyes, somehow thinking I might be mistaken, or it was simply a mannequin that had washed ashore and tangled in the anchor.

No, it was a real person. There was no doubt about it. Crabs scuttled across the corpse, doing unspeakable things to the bloated body, the flesh blue and waxy. The man was overweight, very hairy, and wore a pair of bright pink swimming trunks.

He'd been dead a while and had fared badly. Fishing line was wrapped around his neck, biting into the loose flesh. A hook pierced his chest below the nipple, the line taut as it trailed to a simple black fishing rod wedged upright into the rock beside him.

A fishing trip gone horribly wrong, or something more sinister?

"Hello!" shouted the man fishing just up the coast as he waved and smiled happily, his rod in the other hand.

How had he not seen the corpse? It was right here and as clear as day, but he seemed oblivious. I scrambled to my feet and glanced first one way then the other, but there was nobody around and no way to contact the authorities.

When the fisherman began walking towards us, my heart skipped a beat, and I had absolutely no idea what to do beyond running away.

But to where? And what about the body below me?

Chapter 2

Anxious' hackles sprang to attention faster than a vanlifer spotting a free launderette as he lowered his front legs and growled deeply at the approaching man. No way he couldn't have spotted the body, surely? Was this mystery solved already? Would I be next? Where was everyone? Why were we alone here?

With the corpse still swimming in my vision, I had to wipe the sweat from my eyes. I became acutely aware of my stinging lips, already dry and cracked from the heat and salt as the man called out again and hurried towards us along the sandy path. He was naked above the waist, wore a pair of dirty, faded blue jeans, and was barefoot. Dark, straight hair hung halfway down his tanned back. Skinny, verging on malnourished, he had a pigeon chest and scrawny, stick-like arms, but there was an undeniable strength there, and I knew instantly that he was no tourist.

"Hey," he panted, as he pulled up short before Anxious who gave a warning growl then crawled forward almost on his belly to sniff the man's feet then his legs, before standing, turning to me, and barking an all clear.

"Hey," I said cautiously, eyeing up this stranger warily, noting his long, aquiline nose, his blue eyes, and lined face. I put him at late fifties, but could have been out by ten years either way as I never was good at guessing ages.

"I wanted to warn you about the rocks there. Very unstable. Not the best spot for fishing."

"I don't have a rod," I said, showing my empty hands.

"No, of course not. That was dumb of me. Be careful anyway. Don't go clambering around. You tourists really shouldn't be coming here. It's not the place for you."

"And why is that?" I asked, caught up in this strange drama, realising I had to focus hard on listening to decipher the very strong, almost impenetrable Cornish accent different from any I'd heard on the mainland.

"Because of the rocks, and the tides, and because you don't belong. Now, you may think I'm being unfriendly, but I'm not. Why anyone comes here is a mystery, and that damn John should stop renting his boats, but he won't listen. Everyone comes then goes away disappointed. Nothing to see here. Nothing to do."

"But you live here?"

"Of course I do!" he snapped, glaring at me, his mood suddenly sour. "Daft question. You alright in the head?"

"I'm fine. No, scrap that. I'm not fine."

"Didn't think so. You should go. This isn't the place for you. Or anyone else. Leave us be. Go home."

"I was thinking the exact same thing. But there's an issue."

"Yeah, what's that?" he asked, stepping closer, ignoring Anxious who was so put out that he scratched at the man's legs until he stopped and looked down. "Hello there. Dogs shouldn't be here either," he warned. "Best you leave too. We don't take kindly to your lot peeing on things, and you better not do a massive poo."

Anxious backed away and whined, then looked to me for backup.

"He's tiny. How could he do a massive poo?"

"Looks can be deceiving."

I took a deep breath, then said, "We better start over. Come with me."

I led him off the path and onto the scrub, then right to the edge and pointed down at the corpse covered in crabs. Waves lapped at the pale flesh tinged blue.

"That's just typical! Now I guess someone will have to deal with it. What a bother."

"A bother?" I gasped, turning to him. "You don't seem concerned about a body on the rocks. Do you know who it is?"

"It's Pink."

"What's pink?"

"He is. Or was."

"I don't understand. He's slightly pink from the sun, sure, so he's been there a while, but he's mostly white."

"No, I'm White. He's Pink. Capital letters. It's our names. We're named after our houses. Pink runs the stupid little cafe. We mostly keep to ourselves here. Only the five of us live on the island, plus a few visitors. And you annoying tourists. Guess now it's just the four of us. That'll be nice. A bit quieter."

I stared at him open-mouthed, trying to digest the information and understand why he was so nonchalant about the death. "You don't go by your real names?"

"I am White. That is all. This is how it works on the island. Everyone here is escaping from something. There is no past, only the present. We are colours. We have no baggage. We are free. The island has no name, at least none we recognise. I know over there on the mainland they capitalise it. But this is not The Island. This is the island, nothing more. And now one of us is dead. It's the way of things." He shrugged, then peered down at the body again.

"What now?"

"Guess we better move Pink. Silly sod must have got tangled up whilst fishing. It's our main food. Can't beat fresh fish, although he'd disagree now. He used to love the stuff," laughed White, "but he still had to catch the fish if he wanted to eat. Look at him, all fat and fluffy. Spent a fortune every week at the supermarket, eating junk, but he did love to fish. Most of us do. Keeps us busy. Ah well. I suppose someone else will take his house now."

"How could someone take it? Doesn't he own it? Don't you own yours?" I was so intrigued by the strange setup that I had to ask, despite us both staring at Pink while we spoke.

"Nobody owns the houses. We have the communal boat which everyone has to chip in to maintain, but the houses are for whoever manages to move in. I had to oust this dumb hippy to get my spot. He was easy to scare off, then I moved in and now it's mine for as long as I can keep hold of it. It's a cutthroat business for sure, but well worth it."

"You booted someone out of their home and moved in?" I was aghast, but beyond curious, and found myself desperate to know more.

"Sure. It's a free-for-all." He turned his attention to me, an eyebrow raised, and asked, "Will you help me get Pink up? Better do the decent thing and haul him out of the water. Don't know how he got under the anchor though. It's been there for years and is very heavy. Weird."

"Yes, very," I agreed, trying, and failing, to figure this strange man out. "Um, don't you think it's rather suspicious? I don't want to tell you what to believe, but are we sure this was an accident? I do have a habit of getting embroiled in murder mysteries now and then." Anxious interrupted me by barking politely, so I nodded then told White, "Actually, quite a few. We need to call the police."

"Good luck with that!" White giggled as he scratched his stubble, then explained, "We have no phone signal."

"But you must have a satellite phone. Internet access? How do you check email and get in touch with the outside world?"

"The whole point of living here is to escape that nonsense. There is no satellite phone, no internet, none of that."

"Very funny," I laughed. When White just stared at me like I had a screw loose, I asked, "You're serious? No contact with anyone else? What if there's an accident or you need to call someone?"

"Then we use the boat and go to the mainland to make the call. A few of the others go online, but I don't have a computer or any modern equipment. Now if you idiot tourists would just stay away, it would be perfect. It's the stupid tea room that's the issue. And the public toilets. Brings in the wrong crowd. Should never have been built. Some fool did it back in the sixties and sometimes residents open the cafe. We take turns cleaning the public toilets, which is a hassle I could do without."

Suddenly I recalled the bloody handprint on the door and realised that there was no way it could have been Pink, so told White, "There's blood at the toilets. A handprint. If it isn't Pink's, then whose is it? We need to find everyone who is here and check if anyone else is missing. How do we do that?"

White shook his head and smiled at me, like you would a child, and said, "You really aren't all there, are you? If we want to speak to the others, we knock on their doors. Don't you know anything?"

"I'm flustered, and concerned about there being a murderer on the loose. Aren't you?"

"It was an accident, pure and simple. Pink got himself tangled and fell over, the daft idiot. But I guess you better go and tell the others."

"You aren't coming?"

"No chance. We don't get on. Nobody speaks to each other here."

Now it was my turn to look at him like he was rather a simple fellow. "There are, I mean, were, five of you and you don't talk? How does that work?"

"Very well, actually. We keep to ourselves, live quiet lives. Don't interfere. It's perfect. Suits me."

"I'll go. Maybe someone should use the speedboat and go to the mainland? I can take the rowing boat. But we need to check if everyone else is alright first. Will you help?"

White sighed, glanced back at his fishing spot, then said, "Fine. Let me grab my things. But I'm warning you, I'm not talking to those utter fools. You can do that. Then leave and don't come back. We don't want you here."

"That suits me fine. I wish I'd never come."

Anxious barked in agreement, then we waited while White ambled back to his spot, collected his things, then returned with his rod and a small case for his fishing gear. He led the way for the short walk back to the harbour, past the cafe where the door swung in the wind, then stood by the wall protecting the houses from the sea and shooed me forward with his hands.

The row of houses ran red, white, green, pink, blue, with low front doors and windows painted the same as the ancient stone, and were so narrow I couldn't understand how there could be a room to the right of each door. Nevertheless, I knocked on the red door. When there was no answer, I tried green, but again there was no answer. Next I tried blue and got the same result.

"Try the pink one," encouraged White.

I frowned as I asked, "Why? He's dead. What's the point?"

"Like I said, he's been missing since yesterday, or maybe this morning. Maybe someone moved in."

"If they did, surely you'd have seen them? You all live so close together."

White said nothing, so with Anxious by my side we approached and I knocked. Almost immediately, the door was flung open and I was confronted with the largest man I had ever encountered. At six one, I was dwarfed by his six seven frame as he crouched to exit. I caught a brief glimpse inside and noted that there was no way he could stand up straight inside. The ceiling was lower than my head height, so would be terrible to move around in, and that was before

I realised how wide he was. He squeezed through the doorway then huffed, his round face red from the effort.

"Who are you?" shouted White from right by the harbour wall.

"I'm Pink. What's it to you?" the man growled, wrapping a grey cardigan around his chest, trying to cover a white T-shirt that rode up high over his belly, revealing a thick mat of black hair that made me gag. His black trousers were too short, and he was barefoot, and all I could think was that either he was terrible at shopping or was wearing a dead man's clothes.

"Pink's dead. He's on the beach," called White matter-of-factly.

"I figured he might be a goner. Didn't answer when I knocked, so I let myself in and now I'm Pink."

"Yes, but who are you?" I asked, my head spinning with the utter weirdness of the names, the situation, and the island itself. "Are you a relative of, er, Pink's?"

"I'm his brother, of course. Came to tell him to get lost and let me have the house, but he never showed. Now I know why." The new Pink shrugged, unconcerned, and it made the whole situation even more surreal. Something was very, very wrong with the people here, and I'd only met two so far. What were the rest like? I truly didn't want to find out.

Anxious barked a greeting and Pink's face brightened the moment he spied him sitting beside me. "Hey there, little fella. What are you doing here? The island isn't the place for lovely dogs like you. Careful you don't get eaten." He chuckled to himself as he bent to stroke Anxious, but struggled because of his obesity and gave up after squatting just a little.

Not to miss out on cuddles, Anxious sprang up and was caught with large hands then cradled like a baby and had a tummy rub before new Pink released him and Anxious landed expertly then sat to await whatever came next.

For an awkward moment nobody spoke or moved, so I asked the obvious, "Why aren't you upset about your brother? Can you call the mainland?"

"There's no signal here, and why should I be upset? We haven't spoken for years, and he was an awful man."

"He really was," shouted White. "The worst."

"It's true," agreed Pink. "I hated him. Now I get the house, and good riddance."

"Can you help us get him up from the rocks? He's stuck down there and it will only get worse. We need to alert the authorities, but we should move him. It might be a crime scene, but we should still do it."

I wasn't convinced this new Pink wasn't responsible, but it seemed rather obvious, although these people were so strange that nothing would have surprised me.

"You want my help?" asked Pink dubiously, stretching his cardigan out of what little shape remained.

"Yes. He's your brother. Don't you care at all?"

Pink merely spread his arms; he could take it or leave it. "I guess I could lend a hand. I wish these damn clothes fit better." Again, he mauled the cardigan, ripping under an arm, but he grinned as he finally managed to do up a button.

Against my better judgement, and with White leading the way, I took up the rear to ensure Pink didn't change his mind, and followed the two peculiar men along the path then down the rocks to the body.

Anxious kept back, well aware what was happening here, so once I'd had a quiet word to soothe his concerns, I joined the two men and we stood beside the corpse. The fishing line was so embedded in his neck I made sure not to dwell on it, but the rest of him hadn't fared well with the crabs and the rocks, and he'd clearly become tangled in the anchor after drifting about like a giant fish on a hook. I couldn't figure out how he'd got himself in such a predicament, or how the hook had pierced his chest, but maybe he'd slipped and somehow it had all gone horribly wrong.

"Silly sod never was very good at fishing," noted Pink. "He loved it, and adored this place, but at least there's a bright side."

"Let me guess," I sighed. "You get the cottage."

"Exactly!" he beamed, slapping me so hard on the back that I stumbled forward, lost my footing, and dove straight at the body, and worse yet, the rusty, jagged end of the huge anchor.

I managed to grab hold of it and stopped my fall, but it was close, and left me panting.

"Careful!" warned White as he hauled me up, his grip strong.

"Thanks." I pulled a knife from my pocket, something I always carried as a vanlifer always seemed to need one, then cut the line free from the reel and rod but made no attempt to get it from his neck as it was too ghastly.

"He's going to be tough to move," noted White as I stood and pocketed the knife.

"He's only tiny," laughed Pink. "I always teased him that he needed to grow. Guess he never will now.

"He's huge," I insisted. "Not as tall as me, but twice my weight. But between us we should be able to get him up to the path."

"Waste of time, if you ask me. Leave him for the crabs." Pink prodded his brother with his bare feet, utterly unconcerned.

"We can't do that. It's disrespectful, and if he's dislodged he might never be found. Does he have any other family?"

"What do you think?" asked Pink. "My brother and I are all that's left. Nobody cares he's dead, and nobody would go to a funeral. Unless you would?" he asked White.

"I hated the guy. But this man's right. We should shift him so he doesn't stink out the place. He's right by my favourite fishing spot."

"Yet you didn't notice him," I reminded White. "Even though you were so close."

White said nothing, just shrugged. There was plenty of that going on, and I was at a complete loss how they were so disinterested.

"Let's get this over with." Pink rolled up his sleeves, then with a grunt, he heaved on the anchor and managed to pull it over and free his brother. It fell back onto the rock with a dull clang, causing the crabs to scatter, so I took an arm while White took the other, and Pink took the legs.

Bracing my back, I heaved, surprised the man wasn't heavier as we lifted him off the ground. We sidled back to the low cliff wall then began the arduous job of going up the path. White and I walked backwards, already struggling, but Pink seemed fine and was grinning, which was utterly incongruous.

Luckily, the climb was short, and we made it up onto the path within minutes. White lost his footing and dropped onto his knees, losing his grip on old Pink. The weight was too much for me and I dropped him, too, and the body twisted onto its back, causing new Pink to release the legs.

"I think we can rule out this being an accident," I said as I stared at the strange symbol carved into the flesh of old Pink's back. The short knife lodged to the hilt in the centre of the disturbing markings glinted as the sun caught the silver handle.

"Now that's ruined what was turning out to be a beautiful day," grumbled White.

"And mine," agreed Pink, staring emotionlessly at the corpse.

"I can't say it's been peachy for me," I said, "but now it's time to get back to the mainland and report this to the police."

"No police!" both men warned, and closed in on me.

Chapter 3

I backed up and Anxious growled as he stood beside me, defiant and willing to fight to protect me. "Don't try to stop me," I warned, taking another step back to get some space.

"We said no police. We don't want them crawling all over the place and ruining things. It'll be a total pain."

"He's dead. Someone murdered him. We need to inform the authorities. What else do you think should happen?"

"Chuck him back in?" suggested White.

"Or ignore him. The seagulls will eat him. Crabs too," said Pink.

"You can't be serious?"

"Deadly," said Pink.

I took a moment to study both men, and for the first time they were sweating. Not from effort, but from fear. It was clear neither man wanted to deal with the authorities, and I couldn't hazard a guess about their pasts but clearly they were here for a reason. I wanted to get away from this madness, and fast.

"I'm leaving. Don't try anything dumb." As they sneered and approached, I turned and hurried off with Anxious by my side, trying to put as much distance between them and us as possible. At the cafe, I quickly retrieved my bag then glanced around, pleased to see that White remained with the corpse. Pink, however, was storming toward us, so we sped up and I only turned when he shouted, "No police," but then he entered the house and closed the door. We raced to the jetty, finally free of their craziness, and things felt calmer instantly.

Relaxing a little, I stopped and took a drink of water and looked out to sea. It was so beautiful staring at the still water and the coastline of Cornwall, yet all I had was a nervous knot in the pit of my stomach. Out of all the mysteries I'd been involved in, this was, without doubt, the most peculiar. In fact, it was downright odd, bordering on surreal, and I couldn't figure out this place or its residents at all.

Who steals his brother's property and doesn't care that he was murdered? Who takes on the name of the colour of their house and doesn't talk with their neighbours on an otherwise deserted island? It made no sense and had me utterly out of sorts. We had to go. And now.

After explaining to Anxious that we were leaving in the boat, I scooped up my unprotesting bodyguard then carefully got in, trying not to rock it too much, but almost taking a dive into the blue. Once Anxious was settled, I undid the rope and let out a sharp laugh of relief, the tension vanishing, then wound the rope up. Settling myself, I reached out then almost freaked out as the boat began to drift from the jetty.

"No oars! Anxious, there aren't any oars."

Frantic, I jumped up, grabbed the rope, almost falling into the water as leaning pushed us further out to sea, but I managed to hold on and hauled us back until we bumped into the jetty. With no other choice, I secured the bobbing rowing boat while seagulls teased us from the safety of the air, then picked up Anxious and made the awkward shift from rocking boat to thankfully stable land.

"Sorry about that, but someone's nicked the oars. This is not a good sign. Where are they?" I studied the water but there was no sign of them, then I figured I could take another boat, but the three others were missing their oars too. Someone was definitely involved in sabotage of the most malicious and downright worrying kind.

We were marooned, with no way to escape bar just taking our chances in a boat drifting around the coast. Would someone see us and call the coastguard? Would we be intercepted by someone on a jet ski? What if we weren't spotted? We could end up anywhere. It was too big a risk, and foolhardy to even try, but the alternative might be even more dangerous. If the killer wanted everyone to remain on the island, it certainly wasn't so they could do a surprise picnic and admit their mistake then call the police.

"The speedboat!" I rejoiced, cursing my befuddled brain for not considering it. "We can borrow it and get away from here. Yes, let's do that." With Anxious cradled in my arms, I decided to check if the key was there, as that would make this much easier. A pang of guilt washed over me as in theory this was stealing, but these were desperate times, and I didn't hold out much hope of White letting me have the key and doubted Pink even knew where it was.

It was an easy step up onto the boat, much better than dropping into the rowing boat, but when I got to the controls there was no key to be found. I searched the limited nooks and crannies but came up empty-handed, so there was no choice but to go and find someone and see if I could borrow the key. With a sinking feeling, which was apt considering our position, I stepped down onto the jetty, let Anxious free, then paused for a moment to consider my options.

Either I tried to find a set of keys covertly, which was a nice way of saying I try to nick them without getting caught, or I find someone willing to let me have them. Pink and White were out of the equation, as no way would they help, but so far they were the only people I'd seen. Where were the other three residents, and what about the tourists? Three other boats meant at least three more people, most likely more, so I needed to go and search.

Maybe I should try White first? I hurried back to the houses, no signs of life, then past the cafe with the door still open, and around the bend then stopped, unsure if what I saw was a good thing or a very bad thing. White was still in the same position, standing over the body of the old Pink, with his retrieved fishing gear in his hands. It was disconcerting, and I wondered if this particular case was already solved, but could it be that obvious? He was flaky enough to be a suspect, sure, but so was the new Pink. Should I try to convince a possible murderer to hand over the keys so I could go and get the police?

Yes, I would. It was the fastest option if he agreed, and at least I'd know where I stood. Quite far away, I decided, just in case he tried anything on.

Anxious, brave boy that he was, led the way, although he didn't exactly race towards White. I followed, keeping an eye on the skinny man the whole time.

"What are you doing?" I asked as we stopped a few feet away, the body blocking the path if anyone happened to come tearing along on a bicycle, which I suddenly wondered if they had here. I supposed there would be no real need, and yet for some reason the image stuck in my head. It was the stress.

"Wondering what to do with him. He's in the way. Sometimes I go for a bike ride, and this fat lump is a problem. He needs shoving back over the side, is what I'm thinking."

"No, you can't do that! We just got him up, and look at the state of him. Aren't you worried that someone carved that symbol into his back? Stabbed him? This was no accident. There's a killer on the loose."

"Aye, well, that's as maybe, but he's still in the way. Inconsiderate, is what it is. Always was a pain in the proverbial, and now even dead he's annoying." White's blue eyes flashed angrily as he tapped his rod against old Pink's back.

"Someone nobbled the rowing boats."

"Nobbled? Is that a Midlands thing? That's your accent, right? What's a nobbled?" White's gaze rose until our eyes locked, his intense stare hinting at violence bubbling under the surface, waiting to explode free.

"It means made them useless. Incapacitated. Basically, the oars are gone. Can I borrow the speedboat? Do you have the keys?"

"Of course I have the keys. We all do. It's a communal boat. I told you that. But I ain't letting you have them. Do you even know how to handle a speedboat?"

"How hard can it be? I assume you just steer and use the lever for speed. Um, are there gears?"

"You'd wreck it in a moment. No way. That's our lifeline to the outside world. Not that I ever want to speak to anyone over there." White waved his hand in the general direction of the mainland, then glared, daring me to ask again.

"Then will you take me? We have to do something. Pink, the old Pink, is a mess, and we can't leave him out in this heat. He smells and is in the way. We need to get help, and maybe take him with us."

"He's too heavy to get onto the boat. It was bad enough dragging him up here. I'm beat. Go ask his brother if you want to do that."

"Will you just take me then?"

White glanced at the corpse again, frowned in concentration, then sighed. "Fine, but it better not take too long. I'll drop you back on the mainland, but don't expect me to come with you. The moment you're there, I'm coming straight back here. I don't like the locals, and I just want my peace."

"White, a man's been murdered. There's no escaping that fact. Whatever you might want to happen, he's dead, and the police will investigate. It's inevitable."

"Then I've changed my mind. I can't be involved in that."

"Is it because of your past? Are you on the run?"

"You ask too many questions. Bad ones. Leave me be."

"If we don't report it, the police will take even longer once they do arrive. Better to get this over with today."

White was silent, and for a moment I thought he was going to say no again, but then his shoulders sagged and he nodded. "Come with me." He brushed past us and strode with purpose towards the cottages.

We trailed behind, both of us anxious, and for once the little guy deserved his name. At the gleaming front door, White paused, checked left then right, then stepped back and examined the roof, which I found more disconcerting than anything as what did he expect to happen? Did they all play games with each other like Kato in Pink Panther? Nothing would surprise me any more. With a grunt of satisfaction that no surprises awaited him, White hurriedly pulled a bunch of keys from his pocket attached to a chain that hung low at his hip, before huddling up to the door and unlocking it.

"Quick! Inside!" he hissed, then opened the door enough to squeeze through before grabbing my vest and yanking me in. Anxious leapt over the threshold like it was red hot, then White closed the door slowly and it shut with the gentlest of clicks. "Don't want anyone to know my business," he said by way of explanation.

"Fair enough. Can you get the keys, please, so we can get out of here?"

"Wait here."

I hugged the wall as he squeezed past me in the ridiculously narrow hallway. Stairs led up, again so narrow it was almost comical, and my back began to ache immediately as I had to bend at the knee slightly because of the low ceiling. How on earth did Pink manage? He was like a giant in a doll's house.

Keen to get a better understanding of this strange man's life, I ignored his order and slid along the wall, jonesing to see more of the tiny cottage. The first thing I noted was that it smelled very fishy. Not in a bad way, just that he clearly really enjoyed fishing, judging by the tackle boxes and rods resting against the wall, making it almost impossible to move. The odour of freshly cooked and raw fish increased as I approached the back.

There were no pictures on the white walls. The bare floorboards were painted white, and very slippery, most likely a high gloss paint usually used for skirting boards not floors, but it was pristine. I poked my head around the door to the right to find a spartan living room with a TV taking up the entire wall opposite and a single armchair. Again, it was white, and leather. A white coffee table was empty. That was it. Nothing else at all.

Anxious shrugged, as confused as me, so we completed the very short walk down the hall to the only other room on this level. The kitchen door was open, revealing yet another utterly white room. White counter of granite with the faintest trace of grey veins, high gloss doors matching the floor. Even the sink and tap were white, so was the induction hob, which I didn't even know was a thing. No pictures, no ornaments, no keepsakes of any sort.

It was like the blandest Airbnb you could imagine, without a single item to tell you about the occupant beyond his fishing gear. A glass table with fabric-covered chairs was the only piece of furniture, with a coat rack doubling as somewhere to hang an umbrella, two straw hats, a fisherman's smock, two heavy duty raincoats, and several sets of keys on the last hook.

White was reaching for the keys when we entered, and he turned with a ready scowl on his tanned face, which morphed into a wicked sneer before he grabbed the keys and said, "Let's go. I told you to wait in the hall."

"Sorry. Hey, do you have a small courtyard or a garden? From outside, it looks like the houses are built into the cliff, but I just wondered if that's true. Mind if I take a look?"

I reached for the handle on the incongruous UPVC white door, utterly out of keeping with the style of the front of the house, but White hurried over in two steps and slammed the door shut before I had a chance to take a look, and growled, "This ain't a guided tour. I'm not an estate agent. I said let's go!" He turned me sharply and shoved at my back, so rather than rile him further I retraced my steps, opened the front door and let Anxious dart out first, then followed, pleased to feel the warmth on my skin after the cool interior.

I glanced back past the cafe along the path, knowing that just out of sight a man lay dead in the sun, and someone on this island had murdered him. And they'd done it today. What time had the other tourists arrived? Could they have done it? What had the guy said? That was it! He'd rented the other three boats this morning, and they'd been hired for the day to explore, so it could have been any of them. I needed to speak to them, but more than anything I wanted off this terrible place and to inform the police.

"Move it," grunted White as he checked we were alone then locked the door before marching towards the jetty.

Anxious and I hurried after him, relieved to be finally making our escape. White wasted no time jumping onto the boat and we followed close behind, then settled on the seat. Anxious hopped onto my lap, and curled up with a sigh, so I stroked him and explained what was happening. He closed his eyes and his breathing slowed, but no sooner had he settled and my heart had stopped beating fast than White slammed his fist onto the steering wheel and turned to me, a deep scowl on his face.

"Something wrong?"

"Yes, there's something wrong. Why do you think we haven't got going yet?" he snapped.

"I assumed you had to set things up. I honestly don't know."

"This is why we haven't gone anywhere." White reached down then lifted a tangle of wires attached underneath the controls. "Someone's nobbled the boat. That's the word you used, right? We ain't going anywhere in this. No way can I fix it." He threw the wires down in disgust then marched past us and jumped onto the jetty.

"Wait! We can't give up. Are you sure you can't fix it?"

"Do I look like an electrician? I haven't got a clue what to do with the wires. It's a mess. No way to fix it. It needs a professional, and I am not one. We're done here. You do what you want. I'm going." White lifted an arm and waved as he marched off, leaving us sitting on the useless boat.

"What now?" I asked Anxious, who opened an eye and glanced first at the retreating figure of White, then me, before whining.

"Yes, I think you're right. We need to explore and see if there's another way off. Maybe there are more boats somewhere on the island, or at least spare oars. There must be something we could use. Maybe some long sticks? I'm sure we could make something that will let me row. Come on, let's go."

Yet again, we clambered off a boat and stood on the jetty.

I felt very alone, and very confused. And about as scared as I believed I had the right to be.

Chapter 4

I sipped from my water bottle, the liquid brackish and warm, but it was better than nothing. Anxious had no qualms regards the quality and slurped from the collapsible bowl then pined for more so I gave him the last of it then we wandered over to the cafe and entered, grateful for the cool. There were various drinks in the fridge, but nobody to pay, so I checked the price list on the menu, left the cash on the counter, and took a can of something fizzy which I drank greedily, the sugar rush welcome. With my water bottle topped up from the tap in the kitchen, I took comfort knowing we could stay hydrated.

Suitably refreshed, and feeling more upbeat about things, although I worried about Min waiting for us now as she'd be fretting, and my folks were due to arrive early this evening, too, I decided the best course of action was to hunt down the residents and tourists and try to get some sense from someone, or at least discover a way to escape. Surely someone must have oars or something I could use? I hunted around the cafe, but beyond smashing a table or chair and using a leg, there was nothing suitable.

For a few minutes, I stood with Anxious whining impatiently, trying to come up with a plan of action. I was thrown for a loop, out of my comfort zone, and utterly confounded. Normally, I handled situations with aplomb and a degree of calm, always keeping a level head and noting details, things that weren't quite right, but in this place everything was wrong, and the tension bubbling away was palpable. It was a volcano way past due for a spectacular eruption.

Regaining my self-control, and finally thinking straight, my confidence grew. I'd been through so much since I began vanlife and would get through this. The people may be beyond weird, and more callous than anyone I'd met apart from the murderer I always managed to uncover, but I wouldn't let that sway me. I would not be beaten by this. Maybe this time I wouldn't solve the case, but I certainly refused to be intimidated or forced to act against my will.

How could I make an oar? Maybe with a few pieces of suitable driftwood plus some table legs and string I could cobble something together. Even one oar would do the job, wouldn't it? It would take a while to get back to shore, but it was doable. Yes, I'd hunt for something and make the best of it then get out of here before anything else happened.

Mustering as much calm as I could, doing some breathing exercises and generally getting my scrambled thoughts in order, I was surprised by how much better I felt. You had to see the funny side of this, I told myself repeatedly. It was utterly absurd and the most surreal experience of my life, so I decided to go with it, possibly even embrace it, but you could be sure I'd be watching both our backs.

I searched in the back room, which was sparse bordering on hilarious for a supposed cafe, and wondered if the deceased Pink ever served anything at all beyond what was in the fridge. Why did he even bother to run the cafe? I guess I'd never find out now. The thought of food inevitably turned my thoughts towards cooking, and the likelihood of missing out on a one-pot wonder this evening truly saddened me as I'd had so much fun the last few weeks cooking delightful meals every single night right outside Vee.

"Now I'm missing Vee," I muttered. The more time I spent with my campervan, the more I felt a deep connection to the sixties vehicle. She had become such a big part of my life that she was family now. My home, my ticket to the wilds of the country and the freedom this life afforded, it still came as a daily revelation just how wonderful it was to be a vanlifer and wake up where I chose with the anticipation of new locations, new experiences, and new friends to be made waiting for me down the road.

I certainly had a plethora of new experiences the last few hours, but it wasn't exactly the relaxing trip I'd envisioned when I'd first lowered Anxious into the boat what now felt like half a lifetime ago.

"I'm wasting time here. We need to go," I told my best friend who was now sitting by the door, head cocked, clearly ready to explore.

"Yes, let's go and check out the island. But first I need to get something." I returned to the store room, grabbed a few large tablecloths, then we exited and I took a moment to raise my face to the cheery sun before squaring my shoulders and together Anxious and I took the path that would lead us around the island.

I stopped for a moment at the old Pink's corpse then lay out the tablecloths over his body and tucked them in around him so they wouldn't blow away, then we followed the trail, mindful of any ambush spots, but the way was clear, the path was sound, and we encountered nobody.

The more we walked, and the more the silence enveloped us, the more enjoyable it became. Whereas at first Anxious remained to heel without me asking him to, after a while he grew more inquisitive and with a quick wag and cock of the head to ask if it was alright to explore, he yipped when I nodded then began to investigate what I was fast realising was a truly beautiful island.

He darted back and forth across the path once it swept inland so we weren't right at the edge, investigating the scrub grass that turned lush when away from the worst of the wind, and it wasn't long before I had a spring in my step and a smile on my face. The track was firm, mostly cobbled the entire length, and well-maintained by the locals, so the going was easy. Now and then it would sweep down majestically to a hidden cove or a short stretch of beautiful, pristine beach, and we simply had to investigate.

We became caught up in a dream state, immersed in this silent world devoid of people. Like we were castaways on a deserted island. A man and a dog revelling in the raw majesty of the surrounding environment. It was an almost spiritual experience that left me both giddy yet empty of thought, just walking barefoot across the sand, our footprints the only ones, until I truly felt like we had always lived here. Just us, walking the path, enjoying the solitude of what I now considered our beaches, our island, not a thought in my head, no concerns, no nothing but a total immersion in this magical kingdom Anxious and I had claimed as our own.

We were kings, and we ruled supreme, if only over the crabs and seagulls who were now our friends and subjects.

And then I collapsed on the beach.

No warning, no jitters or rapid heartbeat. Not even a headache.

One minute I was absolutely fine, or thought I was, the next I felt numb and couldn't feel my body. The last thing I remembered thinking was if the crabs would bow before their new masters. Then the sand was somehow getting close to my face, and I only realised I was about to faceplant when it was too late.

Then all was darkness.

Chapter 5

My world was one of blackness and pain. An elephant was sitting on my chest, crushing my ribs. It hurt to breathe, but somehow I knew this was important, no matter the agony it elicited. Why was breathing a thing?

Slowly, the dense fog in my head cleared and I understood that if I wanted to live I must breathe, but boy did it hurt. I wasn't sure if my eyes were open or not, so I lifted my hand and poked, which really hurt as I jammed a finger into my eyeball. Yep, the lids were definitely open alright.

Now, what was the situation? Ah yes, Anxious and I had been walking around the beautiful, majestic island, and we were its new kings.

That was odd. Why did I think that? And come to think of it, how come I'd suddenly believed such a thing? And wasn't there something about the crabs bowing down before their new masters? That wasn't right, surely?

As the last of the confusion drifted away, and I considered recent events, it became evident that there was absolutely no way I should have felt like that. Something was undoubtedly up. When had it begun? Once we'd returned to the cafe and got a drink, filled my bottle from the tap, and had that fizzy drink, then covered up Pink and started walking.

Heatstroke?

Maybe.

How hot had it been?

Not hot enough to cause that.

What then?

"I was drugged!" I shouted.

The world became wet as the load on my chest lightened and my face was soaked in a sticky substance that glued my eyelids shut and went up my nose. Senses on full alert, I laughed heartily and merrily as everything began to make sense.

I reached out, still cautious, and the elephant turned out to be a very small, and rather upbeat dog I knew very well, who was currently licking my face, his tail brushing back and forth against my stomach.

"Anxious, is that you? Please tell me it is. Are you alright? Are you hurt?"

A sharp bark that echoed around what I sensed was a small room confirmed my suspicions and put my mind at ease. I reached out again and stroked his back, comforted by the familiar feel of his short, bristly yet somehow always soft fur. As familiar as my own hair, it eased the rising stress levels. As I calmed, I sat upright and let him slip into my lap where he curled up, seemingly content to remain that way.

The ground was hard, so I wasn't on the beach, which meant after I'd blacked out someone had moved me. No mean feat as I was six one and pretty solid, so how far could I have been carried or dragged? Maybe Pink had merely flung me over his shoulder, or had help from White. It was possible, but didn't ring true.

With little other choice, I asked Anxious to move, then stood, regretting it instantly. I cracked my head badly on the ceiling, and reached up to find it was rough rock, and wet. Slumping back down, I discovered what felt like a camping light with a hook, so managed to find the button eventually and clicked it on.

"A cave? What are we doing in a cave?"

Anxious barked, his voice reverberating around the small rock tomb that elicited claustrophobia. I stood carefully this time, and with the lamp held aloft investigated the small space, noting that it was indeed a damp cave and that there was only one way out. We kept close and approached the opening, which turned sharply and we were immediately in the light. The ground sloped down steeply and soon water lapped at our feet.

The entrance wasn't far, and as I stood there, joyous to see the blue sky and hear seagulls screech, I grew concerned as I recognised the beach, or what little remained uncovered by the tide coming in fast, and realised that if I'd remained where I'd fallen I would have drowned.

"Someone saved us, buddy. We'd have been dead by now otherwise."

The little guy whimpered, the water up to his tummy, so I cradled him and waded through the shallows, onto the slither of remaining sand, then up onto the path before plonking myself down, my legs dangling over the edge of the rocks, and wiped my brow with a shaking hand.

"What is going on here? How were we drugged? This place is beyond freaky." I noted my backpack a few feet away, hanging from a twisted tree, so went and grabbed it then sat as Anxious came over and lay beside me. I opened it up, in need of a drink, but found my water bottle empty and a note wrapped around it. "Don't drink the water!"

Anxious whined.

So did I.

"Someone's looking our for us, buddy. They saved us. How could the water have been tampered with? Whoever drugged us must have put it in my bottle, but when? And why?"

Anxious had no answer, so I tried to think back, and the only time I'd left my bag was when I'd been moving old Pink's body. That meant it was someone else on the island.

"I hate this place!" I lamented, now more convinced than ever that leaving by any means possible was imperative.

Maybe I could swim? How far was it? Too far, I was sure, and what about Anxious? He'd never make it and no way would I leave him behind.

There was nothing for it but to carry on our trek around the island and try to find someone or something that could assist us. After all, we were all in the same boat now, or lack of boat, so surely someone would be as keen as me to figure out a way off this cursed rock.

Time to find out.

Weary, confused, but determined, and feeling rather bashful about the whole king of the crabs thing, I nevertheless stowed the note and my bottle, just in case it was evidence, and with Anxious by my side began walking once more. This time, I had a clear head and got a very different impression of the island. Whereas before I'd seen nothing but unparalleled beauty, now I realised that half the tiny beaches were covered in trash washed ashore. Plastic bottles, old nets, random bits of furniture—it was an eyesore and shameful on so many levels.

The path was rough and uneven, almost gone in places, and had fallen away in several precarious spots; nobody had repaired it. What a shame. It could have been truly stunning, but the more we walked, the more I saw that made me understand this small would-be paradise was seriously neglected and nobody seemed to care.

I missed Min. I missed Vee. I missed sitting outside her in my wonky camping chair and waiting for my dinner to finish bubbling away, then eating on my lap while I watched people enjoying themselves outside their tents. I missed my mad parents, and I really, really missed feeling safe.

"We're halfway around now," I told Anxious as he raced back, tongue lolling, and skidded to a halt beside me. "Let's take these steps up and check out the castle. Maybe everyone's up there. Let's hope so anyway."

Anxious tore off the way I pointed, making me smile despite my misgivings as he was just such a positive, happy guy.

I trailed behind, apprehensive and still trying to figure out how, and why, I'd been poisoned. Maybe it wasn't to kill me, but was a warning. It still meant there was someone on this island who wanted me out of the picture and was a killer. Poor Pink was testament to that.

The steps were in terrible condition, unlike those at the harbour, which was understandable as most would ascend when they arrived off their boat, but for Anxious they held no challenge and with my long legs, and admittedly generous foot size, I had no problems using the trail even in my Crocs.

Approaching from what felt like the wrong side actually turned out to be the right side. The castle had been built as a rather eccentric defensive building to watch out for marauding invaders, meaning as we ascended higher we had an unfettered and truly inspiring view out to the sea with nothing between us and the horizon.

We finally reached the summit to find ourselves on a narrow dirt track circling the outside of the castle remains, a high, looming, dilapidated wall barring our entrance into the castle's interior. It was in poor condition, the mortar eaten away, and seemed very precarious to me. Judging by the number of fallen stones, I was right to be cautious, so continued around to the west, hugging the wall, mindful of the very steep, sheer drop if I missed my footing. What kind of tourist attraction was this? The whole island felt like a death trap.

It was a very short walk around the remaining fortifications before we discovered the entrance, and I stepped inside gratefully, vertigo threatening to overwhelm me.

The wind cut off abruptly and I found myself in a very peculiar situation. I stood inside the grounds, back against the wall, and took in the scene before me. A couple in their fifties were sitting on a red and white striped picnic blanket in the middle of the remains, a large wicker hamper open with various plates, mugs, a flask, sandwiches, and assorted snacks spread out before them. They clinked glasses and sipped, smiling merrily at each other. A half-finished bottle of Cava stood between them, an empty one on its side next to it.

He wore the usual hiking gear of sturdy boots, green waterproof hiking trousers, a nondescript grey shirt, and a utility waistcoat with a lot of pockets, zips, and D-rings for carabiners, the look completed with a floppy grey sun hat. His companion wore almost identical gear, but no hat, her brown hair blowing in the subdued breeze. Both were red-cheeked and glassy-eyed, but seemed to be enjoying themselves immensely as they laughed and chatted in-between guzzling their booze.

At the far end of the enclosure, standing next to the leaning tower, and staring directly at me but saying nothing and making no attempt to acknowledge me, was a man in his thirties wearing black cargo shorts, a faded T-shirt, with a battered rucksack hanging loose in his hand. Lustrous hair matching his all-black clothes and gear shone as the sunlight bounced off the incredibly straight locks running down past his shoulders, and he was very tanned. With a sharp beak of a nose, and thin lips that somehow remained very pale, he reminded me of a crow, his skinny legs and matchstick arms making it impossible not to compare him to a bird.

Directly opposite him was a lady of indeterminate age, possibly late thirties or early forties, who was scribbling away in a notebook, oblivious to everything else. She was five feet at most, overweight but not unduly so, and wore a paisley dress that left her arms bare and stopped just past her knees. Sturdy army boots with red laces completed the look, and I liked her immediately.

Even though she was focused on her writing, she was smiling, her freckled face warm and welcoming, her shock of red hair and pale skin a welcome burst of colour after focusing on the man in black.

I said nothing, just let my eyes drift from one person to the other then back again, and when I locked eyes with the crow man he made an almost imperceptible nod of acknowledgement before his attention drifted away from me to the woman then the couple.

Anxious, confused by the lack of adoration, sat in front of me and wagged, asking in his own special way if he could go and say hello and let them know the best dog in Cornwall had arrived and the party could start.

I chuckled, then said, "Sure, go ahead," and he raced off to the couple and sat before them, tail swishing, and yipped to get their attention.

The chatting, laughing couple paused, drinks halfway to their mouths, and gawped at Anxious for a moment before they smiled and then the woman shrieked merrily, "Look, a lovely Jack Russell. Isn't he adorable, Bob?"

"Really cute, Babs," he agreed, reaching out to stroke Anxious who leaned into it then turned sideways as Babs flung a hand out and patted his head.

Anxious was in his element, generously allowing strangers to stroke him, but I knew his game and as he sneakily twisted, his mouth open and his eyes flaring with mischief, I ran over and snatched him up before he could nab a sandwich and ruin their picnic.

"Sorry about that. He's small, but would devour your grub in seconds." I held Anxious up high until our eyes met and warned, "No stealing food."

Anxious wagged, protesting his innocence.

Laughing, I lowered him and he sat, eyes glued to the fantastic spread on the blanket.

The couple giggled, then finished their drinks before placing them carefully in the hamper and standing, holding on to each other. Swaying, they smiled at me, and Bob introduced himself then Babs, his wife. Both gave me a hearty handshake and were about as nice a couple as you could hope to meet. The Cava had certainly worked its magic, yet I got the impression they were fun folk with or without the alcohol.

"I'm Max, and this is Anxious. And before you say it," I added hurriedly, "it's his name, not his emotional state."

"What a sweet name," said Babs.

"Indeed," agreed Bob. "Let me guess. When he was a puppy he was anxious and you named him, then he became confident but the name had to stay. Am I right?" Bob beamed at me then Anxious.

"You nailed it," I chuckled, warming to them.

"Can we give him a snack?" asked Babs, bending, then grabbing hold of Bob to steady herself as she retrieved a sandwich.

"Sure, as long as you don't mind?"

"We love dogs," said Bob, smiling at Anxious as he sat, eyes interested in only one thing.

Babs gave Anxious his sandwich, and he settled at our feet to enjoy the impromptu meal while we watched for a moment. "We lost our little darling recently, so came away to cheer ourselves up. Cornwall is so beautiful and we've done lots of exploring. Isn't this place so cute? It's got a strange feel to it, but we're enjoying ourselves."

"We sure are. Especially with the bubbly," chuckled Bob, reaching down to retrieve the bottle and glasses. He poured the rest of the Cava into the glasses and they sipped happily.

"Look, I'm sorry to interrupt your trip, but there's an issue and I've been trying to find everyone else who came by boat, and the other residents. It's proving harder than I imagined."

"Nothing too serious, I hope?" asked Babs after a sip.

"I'm afraid it is. Look, can we get the others, then I'll explain?"

"Others? You mean the weird bloke in black and the woman who hasn't stopped writing in her notebook?" asked Bob.

We took a moment to check on them, and the woman was still writing and the man was staring at us from the shadow cast by the tower, but he didn't so much as bat an eyelid to indicate he noticed us.

"Yes, those two. Do you mind? I wouldn't ask if it wasn't extremely important."

"Well, colour me intrigued," chuckled Bob as he finished his drink. Babs necked hers so he took the glasses and returned them to the hamper Anxious was sitting beside, trying to vibe the sandwiches to levitate in the direction of his mouth.

"Excuse me everyone," I shouted. Not my usual style, but I figured it would save time. "Can we gather around here? I have terrible news and you need to hear it."

The man shrugged then sauntered over, his walk wooden and stiff, making him even more bird-like. The woman continued writing, oblivious, so I nodded to the bird man then went over to her and coughed politely. Still nothing. She just wrote and wrote, then flipped the page and continued, unaware of my presence.

"Excuse me?" Nothing. I tapped her on the shoulder and she jumped back, eyes wide in shock, then looked at me before closing her notebook and clutching it tightly.

"Sorry, I was miles away. Caught up in my world," she said, smiling warmly, a quizzical look in her eyes.

"I apologise. I need to have a word with you and the others waiting over there."

She looked in the direction I pointed, then raised an eyebrow and asked, "What about? Is everything okay? Has something happened?"

"I'm afraid it has. Something terrible. I fear it might get worse. Would you mind joining us? This is very important. I'm Max, by the way."

"I'm Isadora. Izzy for short. Which I am. And you're the opposite. Gosh, you're very tall, and, er, muscular. Sorry, sorry, I'm babbling. I get a little flustered with strangers, but sure, I'll come."

"No need to feel flustered. I'm an easy-going guy and I don't bite." I smiled as we shook hands and she relaxed.

We returned to the others and, feeling rather self-conscious, I introduced myself, and Anxious after he barked, so had to explain about his name, then the others introduced themselves to each other. We waited, but when the bird man remained silent, I asked his name.

"Why?"

"So we know what to call you," I said, confused by his reticence.

"Carl. I'm Carl. What's this about? What's the deal with dragging me away from my quiet time?"

"I didn't mean to intrude, but this is important. Maybe the most important thing that's ever happened to any of us."

"Yeah, sure," he grunted, then turned to leave.

"I've just been drugged and nearly killed, someone's stolen the oars for the boats, there's no phone signal, no way to contact the mainland, the speedboat has been nobbled, and a man's been murdered, possibly by someone in a cult or practising black magic, and now his brother has moved into his house and doesn't even care and I can't find the other residents."

Everyone stared at me like I'd grown an extra head, their mouths opening and closing.

The only sound was Anxious rifling through the treats on the picnic blanket, and he turned to me, guilt written large on his tiny face, before grinning and sitting, waiting for the chaos that would surely ensue.

Chapter 6

Carl hissed, "This guy's a total nut job!" then turned to leave again.

"I promise I'm not. Can't you feel it? This place is wrong. It's utterly weird. The residents call themselves after the colour of their houses. I met White, and the old Pink is dead, murdered, and now his brother has taken over the cottage so is called Pink. We had to haul old Pink from under an anchor, and he had fishing line wrapped around his throat. When we got him up onto the path, we found a symbol carved into his back and a knife stuck in. He was murdered."

"You aren't joking?" asked Carl, spinning to me.

"Of course not! This is really serious, and we're stuck. There's no mobile signal, no satellite phone, no internet access, and we're stranded."

"That can't be right. We're not far from the mainland. Phones work from satellites," said Izzy, scribbling in her notebook.

"What are you always writing in that book of yours?" asked Carl. Sauntering over with a cocky swagger, he tried to snatch the book.

Izzy backed off, stowed her book in her bag, and jabbed her pen at him. "You leave me alone! I don't like bullies. I may be short, but I'm not afraid of you."

"Yeah, back off, Carl," said Bob. "Not cool, son."

"Don't you son me. I'm forty-two. You might be a few decades older, but I'm not your son."

"A few decades older!?" blurted Bob. "How dare you! We're both fifty-nine and fitter than you, you skinny freak. You look like a raven, or a sick blackbird. You should eat more."

"What, even though I have IBS?"

Bob reddened, but squared his shoulders and whispered, "Bully."

"I am not a bully, but this chick's freaking me out. What are you writing, eh? Is it about us?"

"No, it's nothing like that. You mind your own business."

"Can we please focus on what I just said?" I asked, exasperated by how quickly this had descended into chaos. "We need to find the other residents, see if they're still alive, and figure out how to get off this island."

Once everyone had checked their phones and realised that at least that part of my tale was true, they agreed we should return to the harbour so I could show them the corpse, much as I had no inclination to do so.

Babs and Bob took a while to clean away the remains of their picnic, and opened a third bottle while they did so. Either the death of their dog had hit them really hard, or they were regular drinkers. For most people, three bottles in the afternoon would have floored them, but they seemed to handle it well enough although both were rather unsteady as Bob carried the hamper and Babs linked her arm through his and they weaved their way towards where we waited at the leaning tower of madness.

"Blimey, look at this pair," said Carl with a sneer. "They're hammered."

"They have drunk almost three bottles," I said.

"They need to rein it in. How were they going to row home? They'd get lost and most likely head off in the wrong direction."

"Not a drinker yourself?" I asked, trying to be chatty.

"I enjoy a drink, but not when I'm in the middle of the sea and have to row back to shore. The climb's steep too. They'll be rolling down the hill, not walking."

Babs and Bob beamed at us as they stopped and Bob dropped the hamper. Something smashed inside but he didn't seem to notice. Babs just grinned at him before taking a hearty sip of wine then frowned as the glass was almost empty so opened the hamper, topped them both up, ignored the broken crockery, and closed the lid.

"We ready to go?" asked Bob, nodding his head like one of those suction cup things you stick on the dashboard.

"What an adventure!" explained Babs. "So much mystery and intrigue and all delivered by a tall, handsome, brooding stranger."

"If anyone's brooding, it's him," interrupted Izzy, pointing a finger at Carl.

"I don't brood. I just don't really like people. They're annoying."

"So are you, mate," laughed Bob as he slapped palms with his wife and they drank to congratulate him on his comeback.

"We should get going," I said. "Anxious, care to lead the way?"

Bewildered by the rising babble of insults and general confusion, he was more than happy to follow scents on the path to the harbour, so led the way with me behind him and the others following in single file down the precarious, narrow steps that weren't in as good condition as those I'd spied lower down.

I feared for the happy couple, but whenever I checked they were smiling merrily and seemed in control, and within ten minutes we arrived by the cafe without any harm coming to anyone.

"Let's grab a drink first," Bob told Babs. "A beer or another bottle would cool us down."

"Oh, good idea," said Babs, rubbing her hands together.

"I wouldn't recommend that," I said. "Remember, I got poisoned and the note said not to drink the water. I filled up from the tap and bought a can of something fizzy, but I can't guarantee something won't happen."

"If it's sealed we're good to go," said Bob, determined to stay upbeat.

"They don't sell alcohol," I said, hoping that would work.

"Don't be daft. Cafes in places like this always sell booze. I'll go ask."

"You can't," I sighed, "Remember, I told you old Pink ran the cafe for a few hours a day but he's dead. There's nobody inside."

"Then I'll leave my cash on the counter. We have real money don't we, Babs?"

"Loads. I prefer cash to those silly cards. You can never keep track of what you spend."

Determined to grab more booze, the wobbly ones rushed inside the cafe, leaving us at a loss.

"We should go in and make sure they don't trash the place," suggested Izzy. "They seem determined to party no matter what."

"They're definitely buzzing," noted Carl with a disinterested shrug.

"I think you're right, Izzy. But remember my note. Don't drink the water. You haven't yet, have you?"

Both shook their heads, so to the sound of banging doors, breaking crockery, and then a shout of victory, we reluctantly entered the peculiar little tea room. What was the difference between that and a cafe? Maybe tea rooms didn't serve food? I couldn't recall seeing much on the menu beyond the usual tea and scones offering and wondered if that counted. Surely it did?

Anxious sniffed, then yipped for joy, and raced through Carl's legs, jumped onto a chair, vaulted onto Izzy's shoulder, which to be fair wasn't that much of a leap, then sprang down into the cafe and slid across the black and white chequered floor and under the counter into the heart of the building.

I gave chase, worried about what he'd get up to, but with Izzy and Carl ahead I had to slow and follow them behind the counter where I came up short and for good reason.

"Wow, these two are some crazy hikers. They look so normal, so boring, but look at them go. It's like two pigs in sh—"

"I get it," I interrupted, unable to take my eyes off the pair of serious boozers.

"Stop it! What are you doing?" screeched Izzy, whipping out her notebook and writing hurriedly.

Bob and Babs looked up from the cupboard they were raiding and asked, "What?"

"You're out of control and stealing? That isn't yours. It isn't even for sale. It's private things. In a cupboard."

"It's just homebrew. Nothing to worry about. Homemade wine. Looks nice," said Bob, grabbing two bottles and adding them to the row already placed on the metal work table in the small commercial kitchen.

"Izzy's right," I said. "That doesn't look like it would ever be for sale. The bottles are re-used, there are no proper labels, just handwritten ones, so maybe it's best if you put it back."

"Maybe he's right, love," conceded Bob, nodding to his wife.

"Sorry, we got rather carried away. This is just such a lovely place and we're having a fab time, so wanted it to carry on. Oh, look over there!" Babs shot up, eyes wide, as she spied a commercial fridge stocked with cans of soft drinks, bottles of water, and yes, small bottles of wine.

"Result!" roared Bob, then hurriedly crammed the homebrew back into the cupboard, shut the door, and joined her.

We waited while they rammed as many bottles as they could into their backpacks, then guided them outside before they did any more damage, but Babs remembered she'd forgotten to pay so went back inside to leave money on the counter then returned.

"Can we please get this utter bore-fest over with?" asked Carl with an exaggerated yawn to prove how disinterested he was.

"Sure. Follow me."

Anxious and I led the way around the bend in the path then stopped before the large tablecloth-covered lump in the way.

"Is he under there?" asked Izzy.

"No, it's just a rock with a blanket covering it." Carl's voice dripped with sarcasm and yet even he was intrigued and nudged the body with his black boot.

"Can we see?" asked Bob, suddenly sobering up, two pinpoints of red brightening on his already flushed face.

"Just so we know you're on the level," said Babs.

I nodded to each of them, then pulled away the cloths to reveal the terrible state of the corpse.

Izzy gasped and made some hurried notes, Carl stepped back and wrinkled his nose then turned away, but Bob and Babs bent to the body and began to study it in minute detail.

"What are you doing?" I asked, squatting beside them and holding my breath.

Anxious whined and backed away then stood beside Izzy, watching as she wrote.

"Checking out the markings. We're both pagans and know quite a lot about the meaning of symbols. They hold power."

"They do," agreed Bob, reaching out to trace the lines.

"So gross," shouted Carl, who had shifted further away.

"It's just flesh. He's dead, sure, but it happens to everyone." Bob continued to trace the symbol, unperturbed by the grisly sight.

"Have you dealt with death before?" I asked, certain they had.

The pair laughed then turned, and Babs said, "Every day. We're morticians. It's our job to make the deceased look their best for their loved ones. We pride ourselves on our work, and we've seen much worse. You get used to it."

"What does it mean?" I asked, shuffling closer despite my misgivings.

"Not sure, but it's interesting for sure. See the circle?"

"Yes, that's obvious."

"It's the circle of life. The never-ending cycle of life, death, and rebirth. Like the serpent eating its own tail. Yin and yang, or any number of combinations."

"Or someone did a bad drawing of an orange," said Carl, who had braved it and stood beside me now.

"No, it's symbolic. And then we have these intersecting lines, and that swirl in the top segment, which is interesting. Then this dagger bisecting the whole thing. And look, the actual knife is thrust right into the centre, which is like ensuring the magic is active. It's hard to make sense of it all, especially with the blood, but this means something." Bob creaked to a standing position then helped Babs up. With a nod, they shifted away and talked amongst themselves for a while before taking out a small bottle of wine each and swigging happily.

I covered the body back up, ensured the tablecloths were tucked in, then joined everyone and asked the morticians, "What do you think this means?"

"That there's a crazed maniac on the loose," said Carl, squinting as he checked back towards the cafe.

"We aren't experts," said Bob, ignoring Carl, "but there was definitely a knife symbol. That means violence."

"Duh," sniffed Carl.

"But as for the other marks, it's impossible to decipher them. It's definitely ritualistic, and they took their time. Most likely, although we're morticians not medical professionals, he was killed by the fishing line then his flesh was carved. The wounds are what you'd expect once blood was no longer pumping. He's been dead half a day or so, so not long."

Silence descended as the obvious question became uppermost in everyone's mind.

Our circle widened as everyone looked at the rest of the group, faces full of concern, although Carl mostly sneered then looked blank.

"When did everyone arrive?" asked Izzy. "I got here just before midday, then went straight up to the castle and have been there ever since. I wandered around it, but mostly sat and enjoyed the view. Bob and Babs, you were already there, and already drinking then, right?"

"Don't judge. We're on holiday."

"I meant you must have arrived before me."

"Oh, yes, we got here about ten and had a lovely walk around the island before heading up there."

"And I got here at just gone twelve," said Carl. "Not that it's anyone's business. What about you, Max?"

"It was about two. I've only been here a few hours, but it feels like I've been here for days. I still haven't seen the other residents though."

"So if Max is telling the truth, it rules him out," said Izzy, taking a note. "But as for the rest of us…"

"Don't you go insinuating that me or Babs did this," mumbled Bob, glancing at Carl then stepping in front of his wife to protect her.

"Hey, I'm no killer," protested Carl.

"You resemble one with your black hair, black clothes, and your bad attitude. You're aloof and not a team player. You look suspicious." Bob spread his arms as if that could ward off Carl if he chose to go on a murder spree.

"That's judgemental. I keep to myself is all."

"Why did you all come here?" I asked.

"Why did you come here, Max?" hissed Carl.

"I've recently become a vanlifer and have been travelling around the country. I've spent a fair amount of time in Wales, then back down south, then here and there. The summer seemed over, so we headed down to Cornwall chasing the last sun and warmth for the year. We've had a fun few weeks and I'd seen the island so wanted to visit. I arranged to meet my ex-wife, and er, my parents back on shore later today. I haven't seen my folks for a while or my ex for a few weeks, so we were going to stay at the campsite I'm at. My folks are getting a hotel."

"You still talk to your ex?" asked Bob. "Good for you."

"Weird, if you ask me," said Carl.

"Actually, it isn't. I screwed up and we got divorced. It's been well over a year now and we're the best of friends. Hopefully, we'll be back together next year, but we try to see each other as much as we can."

"You're that guy!" declared Izzy, making a note. "Max Effort, the man who keeps solving murders. I read about you on one of my forums. I read your wiki page."

"What's this?" asked Babs.

"He's solved loads of murders. Travels around the country helping out communities and solving seemingly inexplicable cases. All the local detectives hate him."

"Not all. Some have been very nice and quite helpful. The last case was like that. My dad called the case Ninjas and Nightmares as it was a murder in a haunted house. Min was there with me."

"Max and Min? That's dumb," grumbled Carl.

"I think it's cool," said Babs.

"You would," said Carl dryly.

"What's that supposed to mean?" demanded Bob.

"I think we're getting sidetracked," I said, trying to get everyone back on the same page. "So, we know the rest of you were here when this happened."

"Although you could be lying," said Izzy, blushing a little. "Not that I'm accusing you, but you could be."

"That's true," I admitted. "But I promise you I'm not. Carl, what's your profession?"

"Musician. I play guitar in quite a well-known band actually. We've just finished up the festival circuit for the year and I'm totally burned out. Come to think of it, your name does ring a bell. Were you at Lydstock?"

"I was. You were there?"

"Sure was. Go every year. We don't get the best slots, but we do alright. It was a fun festival until the murder. Damn, you did solve it, didn't you? I missed the big reveal but heard about it from the guys and loads of others afterwards. Wow, you are on the level."

"I really am. Now, Izzy, what about you? And may I ask why you keep writing in that notebook? I don't mean to pry, but it might help us figure this out if you wrote something relevant."

"I just write about what goes on around me or my thoughts. It's like a diary really. I haven't seen or heard anything here that would help. Just descriptions of the place, things like that."

"And your job? Do you have one?"

Izzy mumbled something but nobody heard her, and everyone asked her to repeat it at the same time.

"I'm a professional mime artist," she shouted, glaring, hands on hips.

Everyone backed away, panicked, eyes darting, and all I could think was that maybe I should try to swim back to shore, consequences be damned.

"Don't worry," she shouted, as we retreated away further, "I won't do any mime."

"Promise?" I asked, fear making my voice waver.

"Yes. I'm not one of those mime artists who performs whenever they have an audience, like some do. I know it's not for everyone, but I make a decent living travelling around and performing at arts festivals and private parties. People really do enjoy it."

"As long as you promise not to do the pretend box or sheet of glass thing," I warned, my heart fluttering.

"Oh, you mean this?"

And so it began.

Why can they never resist?

Chapter 7

We stared in abject horror as the grinning Izzy "mimed" that she was trapped in an invisible box, her squat body crouched low, hands first investigating the roof, then the walls. She somehow found that the ceiling had risen, so stood with an exaggerated look of shock then continued to explore her inexplicable prison.

Beads of sweat pinged to the surface all over my body, even my feet, like thousands of pinpricks, and my heart beat fast, yet I was unable to look away from this most awful of sights.

The others were clearly feeling the same, their attention fixed on Izzy as she opened her eyes wide in surprise as she finally discovered the doorway out of the cell only to encounter another barrier a step away.

Carl had backed away and was shaking his head, trying to forget the terrible sight. His forehead glistened and a tic beneath his eye pulsed dangerously.

Bob and Babs clutched each other tight, moaning quietly to each other, but they couldn't tear their gaze away either.

It was mesmerising in an utterly perverted way. Why did mimes grin so much and act so shocked when they found a way out? Why did they think we believed it? Did they really? Why the gamut of facial expressions and sudden looks of utter surprise and glee when they stepped through a pretend window or closed a door behind them?

Anxious whined from his position at my feet, and did the worst thing possible. He lifted a paw from over his eyes and was stuck watching, howling as Izzy discovered the walls and ceiling were closing in on her and she had to sink low to the ground, frantically searching for an escape.

"Luckily" she discovered a low door, and jumped up, beaming, then shook out her limbs like she'd just run a few miles.

"Well, what do you think?" she asked nervously, looking at each of us in turn. "I know mime isn't for everyone, but it's a real art form."

"Yes, er, very convincing," I said, finding myself clapping enthusiastically.

The others took my cue and Izzy received her slow round of applause with a broad smile as she wiped her brow like the strain was too much for her.

"I really thought you were trapped in a box," said Bob, necking a miniature bottle of wine then searching in his rucksack for another.

"I can do more if you want?" offered Izzy.

"No, no, no," we protested.

"That was plenty," I said diplomatically.

"Sure, I understand. Sorry about that. But you all seemed so interested."

"Did we?" I asked, sure that wasn't the impression any of us had given off.

"Actually, no, you didn't." Izzy's shoulders slumped and she hung her head. "I'm sorry. I know everyone hates mimes and feel like they have to stay and watch and pretend they enjoyed it. It's the curse of the art form. We can't help it. We know how people will react, but do it anyway. I don't know what came over me."

"And you really make a living from mime?" asked Carl, actually showing some compassion.

"Yes, but it isn't easy. I have to travel a fair bit, and the pay isn't great, but I get to do what I love."

"Then that's all that matters," I said kindly, putting my arm around her and giving Izzy a hug.

"Thank you. You're very kind. Um, I guess my timing was a little off, what with the body. Shall we see about the boats?"

"Great idea!" I said with relief. "I've been trying to figure out how to fashion a makeshift oar, but haven't found anything suitable. Let's have a look at the boats and see what everyone thinks."

Keen for a distraction to eradicate the lingering afterimages of Izzy's performance, we hurried towards the harbour, Anxious leading the way. The poor guy was feeling the effects, too, and every so often he'd whine and shake his head to try to dislodge the terrible afterimage.

Within minutes, we were back where this had all begun; it became obvious to the others that I hadn't been exaggerating. The oars were still gone, the speedboat remained nobbled, and there was no way for us to leave.

"What about the blood at the toilets?" asked Izzy, making notes.

"I've been thinking about that, and I can't make sense of it." I scratched at my bushy beard as I thought about it again. "I assumed it was the body of the man we found, the old Pink, but now I'm not so sure. Let me show you."

We approached the public conveniences and I showed everyone the blood on the railing and the handprint on the door. They took their time studying things and going inside to investigate, but as before there was no body and no clues to where this person might have gone next.

We gathered outside and I said, "I can't believe this was from Pink. It's doubtful he was stumbling about then went to the water and was killed there. He must have been attacked where he was found, so either this is just from someone who had a minor accident and went inside to clean up the wound, or we're looking for another body. It could have been the killer getting cleaned up, but that's not what my gut's telling me."

"Then let's split up and investigate," said Bob. "There aren't many places to look. Max, you already walked around the island, right?"

"Not all of it. I went around half, then found the other steps up to the castle and bumped into you guys. We should check out the other side."

"Great idea!" said Babs. "We'll come with you. I don't think we should split up."

"Or me," said Izzy.

"Carl?" I asked.

With a shrug, he said, "Whatever. But yeah, we should probably stick together. Don't want anyone to get murdered."

"That's the spirit," cheered Bob, clinking bottles with Babs.

"Before we go," I said, "can anyone think how we can fashion an oar, preferably two?"

"Sure, that would be easy," said Bob. "We just need a suitable piece of wood and a jigsaw, or even a handsaw if that's all there is. We can cut out the shape. Hell, you could even make do with a short paddle. Anything to get the boats going in the right direction."

"That's what I was thinking. Or even driftwood. But all I've come across are the tables and chairs in the cafe. Think we could break a table apart and use the lengths of wood? Something like that?"

"They aren't real wood. They're fake rubbish covered in plastic coating," said Bob. "But if we can get our hands on a saw that might work. So, where do we find one?"

"We need to ask the residents," I suggested. "But the men I've met so far don't seem too likely to help. Although, if it gets us off the island maybe they will help. We should ask. Maybe start with finding the residents, then check out the island?"

"I think we should make sure there are no more bodies first," said Carl. "We need to know what we're up against before we start trying to ask them for things. Because, let's face it, if we're agreed none of us is the killer, then it's one of them. Max, what was the deal with these guys?"

"White was fishing just up from where I spotted old Pink. He hadn't even noticed the corpse. Mind you, he wasn't concerned either. Didn't seem to care. He's a strange man and was just concerned about tourists. He hates that anyone comes here."

"What about the brother?" asked Izzy.

"Even more strange. Didn't care that his brother was dead at all. They didn't get on. The new Pink just wanted the house. It's a weird system, but apparently anyone can live in the cottages. Nobody owns them. He came to try to convince his brother to let him live there, but when he didn't return he just moved in. It's too nutty."

"And how did the new Pink get here?" asked Babs.

"That's a very good question! I'm not sure. He said he arrived yesterday, and Pink was missing. Nobody has seen him since then. But he wasn't killed until today. What happened in the meantime?"

"Maybe we should go and ask?" suggested Carl.

"I doubt you'll get much from him. He wasn't the chatty sort and didn't even have his own clothes. He was wearing his brother's, and they were too small for him."

"Too small? But old Pink was huge." Carl eyed the pink house nervously, the most emotion he'd shown since we'd met.

"And new Pink is even bigger. I can't imagine why he wants to live in a tiny cottage where he can't even stand up straight. Let's take a look around first. We might find something on the other half of the island. That might make our life easier."

"Even if we can make oars, what about everyone else?" asked Izzy. "Who gets to leave and who stays?"

"Let's worry about that when the time comes. The main thing is that someone goes to get help. This place is clearly dangerous, so I think you had the right idea and we should stay together."

We regrouped, discussed our plan of action in more detail, then decided to stick to the path around the island and cover only as much ground as I hadn't already. It shouldn't take long, and even with Bob and Babs in their increasingly drunken state it should be safe enough if we stuck together.

Carl and I took the lead, but Anxious would hear none of it and insisted he had to take point and scout ahead so he could warn of anything untoward. I gave him a biscuit to say thank you, so he lay down in the path, his chivalry forgotten.

Tutting, but smiling, we forged ahead for a few seconds until he'd wolfed his snack, then he tore off, happy and keen to explore.

Babs and Bob were behind us, chatting away excitedly, seemingly unconcerned about the murder and boat nobbling.

Izzy brought up the rear, taking notes, and thankfully performing zero mime, which was as it should be.

Carl was quiet, and rather sullen, which I'd learned was his default setting, but he wasn't as unfriendly as I'd first believed, and I didn't feel the need to make chit-chat.

The path was in better condition on this side, although I didn't know why, so the going was easy and relatively smooth over the ancient cobbles. Anxious zipped back and forth, reporting in then dashing off again, and it lifted my spirits. A staccato bark stopped me dead in my tracks, though, and when he tore back with his tail down and his ears tucked low I knew there was trouble ahead.

I asked the others to wait while I went to check on things, but they insisted on coming, so together we followed Anxious as he rounded a bend then dashed through the short grass. We followed, but when a rabbit burst from the undergrowth and he grinned at me, I had to laugh.

"False alarm," I declared.

Anxious returned a minute later, having lost his quarry, leaving me wondering how rabbits managed to survive on such a small island. Maybe someone had kept them as pets and they'd escaped. Surely the population would die out otherwise?

We returned to the path, but Anxious repeated his warning, so we followed him then stopped, our way barred by what appeared to be a scarecrow. Blocking the path was a raggedy mess of a thing tied to a makeshift cross of sturdy poles. The arms were parallel to the ground, the legs tied together, the head hanging down, obscuring any features.

It was clear immediately that this was no pretend man designed to scare off birds, but a real life human being.

"Think he's still alive?" asked Carl.

"We need to check, but I doubt it." I patted Anxious as he sat before the strange sight, then checked the coast was clear before stepping up to the man. A red and black chequered shirt was torn and ragged, his blue jeans ripped at the knees. He was barefoot.

Cautiously, I lifted his head and stared into the lifeless eyes of a man in his early forties. He was clean-shaven, had a short crop of curly brown hair, and a rather lined face. His jaw hung open, revealing incredibly white teeth, and I couldn't help noticing that his fingernails were manicured, although several were chipped, meaning he'd most likely been involved in a struggle. His hands were also covered in blood. Was this the man who'd made the handprint?

The cause of death was obvious. His throat had been slit from ear to ear, then someone had carved the same symbol as on old Pink into his upper chest right below his Adam's apple.

Nevertheless, I checked for a pulse just in case, but knew it was fruitless.

"He's dead," I told the others, then stood aside so they could take a look for themselves.

"Most likely no longer than a few hours, judging by the wound and state of the blood on the ground. He wasn't moved after his throat was slit, so he was probably tied up then killed right here," said Bob matter-of-factly.

"Anyone could have seen," gasped Izzy. "What is wrong with the people here? Who is this guy?"

"No idea," I admitted. "Maybe one of the residents, as there are no other boats. But we still don't know how new Pink got here yesterday. Where's the boat he used?"

"Maybe he had a ride with this guy," suggested Babs.

"That still doesn't explain the lack of another boat. Maybe they moored it somewhere else. We should check." My excitement began to grow, as how else did the deceased get here, assuming this wasn't a resident? Maybe he was. Maybe new Pink came on the speedboat with this man. That would make sense. We needed to figure this out as our lives might depend on it.

Reluctant to leave the body where it was as it felt disrespectful, we nevertheless continued our search of the island but came up with nothing. No more corpses, no boats, no sign of anything concerning.

When we returned to the body, Babs and Bob did a thorough inspection and pointed out the man's bloody hands and suggested maybe it was his handprint on the door. It made sense, but didn't explain how his killer had managed to lure him to this spot then tie him up before murdering him. As before, both morticians insisted the carving of the flesh was performed after the man was deceased.

Nobody had any idea why, though, beyond it being a crazed ritualistic killing of some kind.

Izzy spent a good ten minutes copying the symbol into her notebook, and only then did she agree to return to the harbour so we could try to find some residents.

"Wait! We need to go back," I said, stopping suddenly and annoyed I hadn't thought of it earlier.

"What for? The guy's dead."

"We shouldn't have just moved him onto the grass. We should have untied him."

"The police will want to see him how he is. We won't contaminate the crime scene as much," said Carl.

"I know, but those poles are about the closest thing we have to oars. We haven't found anything else that even comes close, so let's go and get them. We could tie something to the ends for paddles or use them as they are. It's better than nothing."

"He's right," agreed Bob. "Tie something flat to the end and you have a paddle of sorts. It means we can get out of here."

"Let's do it!" screeched Babs, her voice high as the booze level increased.

Despite our reluctance to touch the man, Carl and I nevertheless managed to untie the tight knots with as much respect as we could manage. Grabbing a pole each, we hurried to the others waiting on the path.

Staffs in hand, we led the way back to the harbour and sat on the wall with our feet dangling above the water, each of us lost to our own thoughts, or in the case of Babs and Bob, their wine and not much else.

The pair were like a bottomless pit when it came to the booze. This clearly wasn't unusual behaviour as no way could I even come close to matching them as I hadn't built up the tolerance.

Carl asked if he could have a small bottle of wine and they happily obliged, which I found strangely touching, then they offered one to everyone else, insisting they had plenty and there was more in the cafe anyway.

So there we sat, sipping on warm wine, staring out to sea or looking at the bobbing boats we still didn't know if we could use to escape murder island.

When the wine was gone, and with the effects more powerful than I'd anticipated even though it only equated to a large glass, I got to my feet and asked the others, "Shall we knock on a few doors? See if Pink or White can help, or if the others have returned?"

Everyone agreed it was time, so we got ourselves together then turned and faced the houses.

Would they help, or were we about to come face-to-face with the killer?

Chapter 8

Encouraged by the others, and with them insisting it was best if I knocked because I'd already met several residents, I did as requested and decided to try the doors in order from left to right. First was the red house.

There was no answer.

Next was white.

After a long wait, White did actually open the door. He took one look at me, then glanced over my shoulder at the others before slamming the door shut in my face. I knocked again, and he just shouted for me to go away, but there was no way I'd leave it at that. Especially now.

"What?" he asked, flinging the door open.

"There's another body. A man in his forties with short, curly brown hair, a check shirt, and jeans. He was tied up like a scarecrow."

"Then you better bugger off before one of you is next, hadn't you?"

"How are we meant to do that? How can we leave? Aren't you concerned? How do you expect to get out of here?"

"I don't want to leave. Don't you understand? I can fish, and live off what I have stored in my pantry for months. Sooner or later, someone will come. Now leave me alone. For all I know one of you is the murderer."

"What about this other body? Does he sound familiar?"

"There's nobody else like that here. He's not a resident. Must be a tourist."

"But there aren't any other boats. How did he get here? How did the new Pink get here?"

"Why don't you ask him?" With a final scowl at me, then the others, he shut the door again, but softly.

"He wasn't very friendly," said Izzy, tutting as she updated her book.

"I told you he wouldn't be. Let's try the next one. Maybe green's our lucky colour." Not holding out much hope, I knocked anyway, surprised when the door was opened almost instantly by the strangest woman I had ever seen in my life.

"Hello, dearie. Oh, I see you brought your friends with you. Come in, come in. Don't just stand there gawping," she laughed, retreating inside.

I turned and shrugged at the others, and they repeated the action. Either we went in and took our chances, or we remained outside. Everyone nodded, so with Anxious by my side, then darting in as a glorious smell hit our noses, I stepped inside the cool interior of the tiny green cottage, hoping I'd make it back out again.

"Wow, it's so green," gasped Carl as he entered behind me.

I turned and explained, "The white house was all white inside. I wasn't sure if they all followed the same colour code, but it looks like they do. Weird they don't all dress in the same colours, too, but this lady clearly does."

"It's making me feel queasy," whined Izzy as she entered behind Carl.

With the narrow hallway now full, I followed the current resident into the kitchen to make space for Bob and Babs, wondering what to expect, hoping it was nothing murderous. What choice did we have though?

Anxious was sitting next to Green, tail swishing, eyes fixed on her as she stirred a pot on an old two-ring gas hob. The orange pipe that trailed from it to the blue gas cylinder was utterly out of place in what was otherwise an entirely green kitchen.

Just like the hall, the walls were painted pale green, the bare floorboards dark green, and the ceiling a much lighter shade, which was clever as it made it seem higher than it was. Not that it mattered for Green, as she was shorter than Izzy, but that was where the comparison ended. As Green turned and beamed at us, then returned to her cooking, I saw enough of her to guess she was mid-sixties. She wore all green, and that included her shockingly bright hair.

Her outfit consisted of a pair of simple slippers on her tiny feet and flared jeans that made her skinny frame seem even slimmer. A loose blouse hung off her shoulders like it was on a coat hanger. She had a friendly face, with a ready smile, and clearly spent plenty of time outdoors judging by her tan and deeply etched wrinkles.

As the others shuffled in behind me and murmured quietly about the house, I checked out the compact kitchen just like in White's house. The size was the same, but that was where the similarities ended. Whereas his was modern and pristine, this place was like an Aladdin's cave of curiosities. All the furniture was green, even the old pine table and the dresser that housed mismatched but colour-coordinated crockery, but on the bookcase there were endless books with the inevitable array of colours. They were piled up everywhere in stacks, but they weren't what immediately caught my attention.

Crystals, dream catchers, driftwood, rocks of all sizes, a collection of at least ten umbrellas, a pile of raincoats, Wellington boots in far too many sizes to be of any use to Green, and hats in random places, including at least five on the kitchen counter, meant the place was enough to make me feel unwell. Having always appreciated order and minimalism in most things, this brought out my OCD in a big way. How could anyone hope to stay sane living like this?

I knew lots of people were one pile of newspapers away from being classed as hoarders, and enjoyed the comfort their things brought them, but when it came to the kitchen, and the vast array of items on the counter, it gave me the shivers. How could she clean the surfaces? What about her green sink and tap? There was a stuffed bird next to it, and it was looking at me funny, so I let my eyes drift along the counter and noted a toaster with a crystal ball sat atop it, a feather sticking out of the kettle, and more incense sticks and holders than could be good for your health.

"Now, what can I do for you?" asked Green as she turned from her pot, spread her arms, sauce dripping from the spoon into the gaping maw of Anxious who licked his lips, then smiled at us. "Would you like some supper? Are you hungry?"

"No thank you," I said, figuring it was best not to risk it although it smelled delicious.

"I could eat," said Babs.

"Remember about the poisoning," Bob reminded her.

"Oh yes. Oops, I forgot. I think I'm a teensy, tiny bit tipsy."

"Really?" asked Carl, dripping sarcasm.

"Let me introduce everyone," I offered. After I'd done so, Green smiled, but said nothing.

"Are you Green?" asked Carl, looking exasperated.

"Why yes, I suppose I am. I do love the colour."

"He meant your name? Do you go by the colour of your house like the others?"

"We all do, dearie. It's how we do things on the island. Now, I'm not saying it isn't lovely to have guests, especially because you aren't my neighbours, who are utterly awful people, but why are you here? Tourists, I know that much. But why call on me?"

"We were hoping you could help. I spoke to White and the new Pink earlier and—"

"There's a new Pink? Oh, how exciting. A nice person, I hope, as the others are twisted sickos."

Everyone gasped, and even Anxious whined, as this was not the language we'd come to expect from this sweet, if rather odd, lady.

"Why do you say that?" I asked.

"Because they are. None of us speak, and for good reason. They've all got terrible pasts, I'm sure of it. I'm the only one who has been here for any real length of time. The rest are just newbies. Running from their pasts, I know that much, and we hate each other, I'm afraid."

"Why? What happened so you don't get on?"

"Oh, who even remembers now?" she chuckled, then stirred her pot before repeating her earlier action and Anxious got a few extra drips of sauce. "It's a while back and my memory isn't what it used to be. Now I spend my time either cooking or practising my art."

"You're a painter?" I inquired.

"No, silly. I'm a witch. I practice my witchcraft."

"A witch!" screeched Izzy, then dashed for the door to the hall. "So you killed them?"

"Killed who, dearie? Is she alright? What's wrong with her? Never heard of a witch before? It's quite common these days."

"We found two corpses, and both had a symbol carved into them. One of the men was Pink, and I dragged him up from the water with White, but he didn't care, and neither did his brother, the new Pink. He was even less interested. And just now we found another body, but we don't know if it was your neighbour or not."

"Do you have photos?" she asked, eyes lighting up. With the spoon forgotten and just dropped into the pot, she approached me, then looked up into my eyes. I saw no malevolence there, just interest, but she wasn't even perturbed, let alone concerned, by the deaths.

"I do. They're quite gruesome, but if you could take a look and tell us if the man we found was a neighbour that would be helpful."

I swiped through the various images I'd taken, pausing when she asked, and enlarging them when she admitted she didn't know how to, and she spent a lot of time looking at the symbols. When she'd finished, I pocketed my phone and waited for her to speak.

Rather than do so, she returned to her pot, stirred then tasted it, grunted in satisfaction, then asked, "Are you sure you won't have any? I'm about to eat and you'll have to excuse me, but I'm starving."

"You go right ahead, but we'll pass for now. There's more to tell, and it's put us off eating or drinking anything unless it's from a sealed bottle."

"Suit yourselves. Join me at the table then." Green served a generous helping in a large, chipped bowl, retrieved a small loaf from the oven where she'd left it to warm, then carried it over to the table. She swept books and assorted clothes aside, told us to remove whatever was on the chairs and pile it up somewhere, then settled herself.

We joined her, apart from Bob who stood behind Babs as there were no more seats, then she began to eat as though she were alone. At least I assumed so because it was utterly disgusting. She ate like a starving wild animal, with zero concern for manners or how much mess she made.

This extremely eccentric woman tore into the bread manically, stuffing her mouth full to the brim but forcing in her lovely smelling stew regardless. Spoon after spoon, chunk after chunk, bits spilling everywhere, including all over the floor where Anxious sat merrily hoovering them up with delight. It was mesmerising and utterly confusing. I had never seen anyone eat like this in my life, and judging by the slack jaws of the others and the way Izzy kept putting her hands over her eyes but then removing them as it was so addictive to watch, my new friends clearly felt the same way.

Several minutes later, and with not a word said in the meantime, Green wiped her mouth with the back of her hand, picked up the bowl and licked it clean, then rubbed the remains of the loaf over her teeth as if that would clean them. As a finale, and whilst grinning to herself with unfocused eyes she simply flung the bowl over her shoulder.

It crashed to the floor and broke into several large pieces. The sound of it was so shocking, the act so deranged and ridiculous, that nobody knew what to do beyond stare at her in utter shock.

"Now, what did you say you wanted again?"

"Do you have an oar?" I asked, wishing I could be anywhere but here.

"An oar? For a boat, you mean?"

"Yes, for a boat."

"Of course I do. We have the speedboat and everyone has keys. That's the rule of the island, but I always take an oar with me just in case I get stranded. Actually, I have two. What do you want them for?"

Relief washed over me and everyone whooped for joy as I said, "Someone stole the oars from our hire boats, and the speedboat has been purposely ruined. They pulled the wires out."

"Who did, dearie?" she asked, seemingly unconcerned.

"Whoever killed your neighbours," I explained calmly, feeling exasperated but trying to hide it.

"Don't get snappy!" she warned.

"I wasn't being snappy," I said with a nice smile.

"Good. Now, where did I put the oars? They're around here somewhere."

"Don't you have a shed or something?" asked Carl. "Surely everyone has somewhere else to store things? There isn't much room in these two up, two down cottages."

"Who needs more than four rooms in a house?" tutted Green. "Let me go and have a look in the living room. You wait here and see if you can find them. I do get rather carried away with my collecting, but I'm not a hoarder."

We agreed hurriedly that of course she wasn't, then she tottered off, trailing crumbs, with Anxious on her heels snaffling bits of bread and the odd lump of meat from her stew.

"She's a witch!" exclaimed Babs when Green began banging about in the living room. "She knows what the symbol is, and isn't telling."

"We don't know that," I said, glancing at the open door in case she returned.

"If she practices witchcraft, whatever that means, then she's a suspect," insisted Babs.

"She's right," agreed Bob.

The others murmured their agreement, and Izzy made copious notes as I tried to think things through.

"If it was her, why say she's a witch? She knows the symbols mean something, so why bother telling us?"

"Why?" asked Carl. "Because she's crazy. Did you see her eating? That isn't normal. It was freaky, man. Who eats like that? It was disturbing. Let's get out of here."

"If she's got oars, we need them," I reminded everyone. "And so far she seems harmless. Kooky, sure, but not dangerous."

"Are you certain about that?" asked Izzy, sucking on the end of her pen.

"Actually, I'm not. I agree she isn't you regular person, but I don't think anyone on this island is normal. She's right about one thing. The residents are trying to escape their past. That's obvious with White and this new Pink, and I suspect the same for his dead brother. We still haven't met Red or Blue, so maybe we should ask her who they are and where she was today? There aren't many places she could have been, but something's going on around here."

"That's obvious. Two men are dead," Carl reminded me in his usual bored monotone.

"I don't like it in here," whined Babs, looking a little worse for wear.

"Have a drink, love. That'll calm your nerves."

"Great idea!" Babs perked up immediately and took the offered bottle then unscrewed the cap.

"Are you sure that's a sensible idea?" I asked diplomatically. "If you aren't feeling well, maybe it's the wine making you feel that way."

Both looked at me like I'd lost my marbles and Bob said, "What are you talking about? Why would the wine make her feel unwell? I feel great."

"You can't even stand straight," said Carl. "You're both drunk. There's a murderer on the loose, we're in this weird house with a mad old witch dressed in green, and Babs feels ill so your answer is more wine?"

"I think it's a fabulous idea," said Babs, beaming at her husband then swigging merrily.

"Me too," agreed Bob, taking a drink from his own miniature bottle.

There was clearly no getting through to them, so I turned my attention to the room and began searching for the oars. Everyone took the hint and checked around, but even with all the junk it became clear almost immediately that they weren't here.

"Maybe they're outside," I suggested. "White was weird about me looking out the back, but maybe Green won't mind."

"Why bother asking? Let's take a look." Carl went over and turned the handle on the UPVC door that matched the one in White's house, but just as he did so Green returned and began screeching in a peculiar high-pitched way and batted at Carl with a large oar after dropping the other one.

"Hey, what are you doing?"

"There's nothing out there and I don't want the cold getting in. It's really shady in the back, and anyway there's no garden and I don't store things out there. We're right by the cliff, you know. Here's your oar, now out you go. Go on, shoo. I have things to do. A witch's work is never done." Green thrust the oar at Carl, kicked the other one over to me, and scowled as we assembled by the counter.

"Thanks for the oars, and sorry to intrude," I said.

"Be sure you bring them back. I need them."

"Okay," I said, having no idea how that would work. "But Green, why aren't you upset about what's going on here?"

"Dearie, when you've lived on this island as long as I have, nothing surprises you. People come here for all sorts of reasons, and not all of them good. I don't like my neighbours, but I can't see any of them being killers. It's most likely some idiot from the mainland causing trouble. After all, the scarecrow corpse isn't from here, so how did he get here, eh? There's something else going on and I for one am staying in my cottage where it's safe until this all blows over."

"Good idea. Thanks for the oars. We'll see ourselves out."

"You will not! I want to make sure you all leave, so follow me." Green barged past Babs and a giggling Bob then into the hall where she stood pinned against the wall until we filed out.

"Thanks once ag—"

Green slammed the door shut.

"Let's go home," said Carl.

"Agreed."

None of us could get to the boats fast enough.

Chapter 9

"Shouldn't we have a word with the others in the cottages?" asked Izzy as she ran beside me. "We should warn them."

I slowed, then stopped, and agreed, "You're right. We should." I called to the others but they were loath to take the time, so Izzy and I hurried back and knocked on the doors. To my shame, I was relieved when nobody answered.

"At least we tried."

"We did. Now let's get out of here." I nodded to her, and she nodded back, then we raced to the jetty like our lives depended on it. I got the feeling that they did.

Babs and Bob were bickering as he helped her into the boat. Carl was standing by, watching without emotion, but turned to me as we caught up.

"They're gonna take a dive over the side if they carry on like that. Hey, watch the oar!" He ran to the boat and grabbed the oar from Bob's hand just before he dropped it over the side.

"Oops," he laughed, then jumped in and settled himself next to Babs on the bench seat. "Right, hand me the oar. Max, give me the other one."

Carl took a step back, the oar held upright in front of him like a defence against Bob's rudeness. "No way. Who said you guys got to get in first? What about everyone else? Nobody said you were going. You're both too drunk to even know which way to go. If anyone should go, it should be me and Max. No offence, Izzy."

"None taken, I'm sure." Her body language told another story entirely, but he did have a point.

"Guys, Carl is right," I said. "Do you even know where to go? And what about the rest of us? Maybe Carl and I should go. We'll be faster, and that way everyone gets saved sooner."

"We know the way," slurred Babs, her eyelids heavy. "It's over there, right?" She waved her hand around in a half circle, then slumped sideways, causing the boat to rock violently.

"Careful, love," warned Bob, grabbing her and righting the now almost comatose woman.

"I'm fine. Just stressed," she laughed, her cheeks burning bright.

"I think you both need to get out and let us go," I repeated. "Bob, look me in the eye and tell me you know what you're doing."

Bob glanced up from his wife, but seemed unable to focus properly, and rather than meet my eye he looked at Carl and frowned. "Did you say something?"

"Geez, this pair are absolutely hammered," sighed Carl. "Come on you two, out of the boat. Max and I will take Izzy and you can wait at the harbour."

"We can't do that," I said, much as I wished we could. "They'll fall asleep and anything could happen. We need to stick together. I know it'll be tough, but we can tie two boats together. That way, at least we'll be off the island. What do you think?"

"Fine," grumbled Carl. "But if this pair of jokers keep moving about like that they're going to get us drowned. Can't you be still?" he shouted.

Babs and Bob giggled, then steadied each other and sat, motionless, before bursting out laughing and doubling over then rolling around like landed fish.

"I give up. This is a lost cause."

"Let's just tie the boats together and I imagine in a few minutes they'll settle and fall fast asleep," I said, noting how they were already calming and their eyelids kept fluttering.

"This is on you, Max. I'd rather it was just us three, but I guess we should try to stop them getting murdered."

"That's the spirit," I laughed, hope returning as however hard this would be, at least we were doing something and would soon be heading, albeit slowly, back to civilisation.

Rope was the one thing in plentiful supply, so Carl and I gathered a few decent lengths and then he tied one boat to another, while the two drunks calmed then were still. By the time he'd finished, they were fast asleep and snoring.

"Are we going to do this?" asked Izzy. "Think we'll make it back?"

"Of course we will. It will be slow going with the extra weight, but between the three of us, we'll be fine. We can take in turns rowing so it won't be too tiring, and in no time this will all be over."

"Oh, thank God. This is the most stressful thing that's ever happened to me."

"Me too," agreed Carl.

Both turned and looked at me, so I admitted, "I've had worse."

"Really?" asked Izzy, making a note. "Do tell."

"I've been involved in plenty of murders, and there have been a few that have been so scary as I got attacked a couple of times. But come to think of it, I guess that, yes, this is the worst one. Are we good to go?"

Everyone was, so we gathered our things and readied to get into the lead boat so we could tow the other behind us.

Anxious let out a warning bark, and I turned from my pack I was about to grab to find him right at the edge of the water and barking furiously at Babs and Bob.

"What's got into you? We're almost ready. Calm down."

Anxious turned, then faced the boat again and barked even louder, his tail still and down.

We moved beside him and gasped as we noted the water pooling in the bottom of the boat, already halfway to covering the sleeping couple. The vessel was getting lower in the water by the second, and soon it would spill over the sides and they'd be gone.

"They're about the dumbest people I've ever met," growled Carl. "Should we let them drown?"

"It's tempting," I half-joked, annoyed by their drunken state but knowing I'd never leave anyone in distress.

Wasting no time, I stripped down to my boxers then jumped into the boat and shook them both vigorously whilst shouting right in their ears. Both grumbled and tried to turn over, but either the water or my bellowing got through and they stirred, groggy and bewildered, most likely not even remembering they were in a boat.

"Come on, get out. We're sinking."

And we were. With my added weight, the leak was like a river pouring into the boat and as they sat their legs were submerged. I helped Babs to stand, but she was glassy-eyed and confused. "Bob, you need to stand," I insisted, grabbing him. "Carl, help Babs out. Babs, take it slow and don't make any sudden movements. Do you understand?" I took her by the shoulders and looked into her eyes. Something snapped and she nodded, suddenly frightened.

"Don't let us drown. My Bob doesn't want to drown."

"And you do?" called Carl from the shore, looking bored and frustrated at the same time.

"Eh?" Babs was losing it again, eyes fluttering, so I used the rope to steady myself then shuffled Babs over to where Carl and Izzy each held out a hand. They hauled her out, with a little help from me, and she collapsed in a soggy pile on the jetty, while I turned my attention to Bob.

"Hurry up, Bob, we're about to go under."

But it was too late, and the water breached the side of the boat. We began to sink rapidly. Thinking clearly, I untied the rope securing the lead boat to ours, so it wouldn't be dragged under, but it wasted valuable seconds and now the boat was fully submerged and we were in the water up to our waist.

"Here's the rope," shouted Izzy as she flung it out to me.

"Thanks." I took hold of it then hurriedly tied it around Bob's waist as he protested drunkenly, then told the others to reel him in.

They heaved, and Bob was yanked from the water and skating along before sinking again. With nothing to lose, I abandoned my position and paddled over, turned Bob around so he was floating on his back, then held his head above water with one arm while I reached out for the jetty with the other. I took hold of the other dangling rope and heaved, pulled Bob close, then asked the others to help.

With a shove from me, and plenty of effort from Carl and Izzy, they managed to drag him over the side just as he came to enough to lock shaking fingers on to them, then I used a set of steps to clamber out and collapsed on the jetty, coughing and spluttering, annoyed they'd been too drunk to help themselves, but pleased we'd managed to rescue them.

"The other boat's sinking too," warned Izzy.

Exhausted, but knowing I had to act, I clambered to my feet while Anxious licked me worriedly. I told him I was fine and he relaxed a little, but the excitement still meant he was running about and barking, adding to the confusion.

"Why is it sinking?" I wondered, watching as the boat we were to leave in filled with water.

"The hole in the bottom?" suggested Carl. "I saw it in the one that just sank, and look, you can see it there."

Sure enough, there was a hole in the bottom of the boat, and there was nothing we could do to stop it letting the water in.

"Our weight must have forced the water through faster," I sighed, rubbing at my beard then flicking my hair from my eyes. "Someone's done it on purpose. What about the other one?"

We shifted along the jetty to check on the one remaining row boat, only to find that it was worse than the other one and about to sink. We stood in silence and watched as it was lost to the sea, never to be seen again. Returning to the remaining boat, it was a sombre affair as it, too, sank into the murky depths, our lifeline gone for good, along with our hope of leaving this cursed rock.

"We're well and truly scuppered now," noted Carl. "Two oars, but no boats. The speed boat is too big to stand a chance of getting it to move with just the oars, so we're done for. I've had it with this place. I'm going to swim back to the mainland. It's not far. I can make it."

"You won't. It's too far. You'll end up drowning. How far have you ever swum in your life?" I asked.

"Dunno," he shrugged. "A few lengths in the pool years ago, I guess. Yeah, you're right, I'd be exhausted in a few minutes and be dead." Carl sat on the jetty and dragged his hair behind his back, then stared out to sea, defeated like the rest of us.

Izzy, Anxious, and I joined him and Bob and Babs soon followed. We sat in silence, watching the bubbles surface where the boats had sunk.

"Thanks for saving us," mumbled Bob. "And sorry about the drinking. We pushed things too far, but we're just so damn sad about losing our dog, and, er, we do like a drink even when we aren't sad."

"Yes, thank you all so much," said Babs. "And especially you, Max. You're a true hero. You saved my Bob."

"Think nothing of it. I wouldn't let you drown."

"Bet you thought about it, though, eh?" said Bob, nudging me and winking. "Sorry again. So, what happened?"

"Someone made holes in the boats. Maybe they figured we'd find oars or try to get away without them, so did this to ensure we couldn't escape," I suggested. "It certainly isn't a coincidence. We're on their radar and they're after us. We need to act as a team and find somewhere to stay for the night. No going off alone, and absolutely no trying to swim to the mainland."

Everyone agreed that was the last thing they were considering as it was too far, and then the discussion turned to what we should do and what our options were. They were limited, very limited, and beyond just hunkering down for the night I had no suggestions. We needed to find a way to escape, but now that seemed very unlikely.

"The only thing to do is wait for help to arrive. Maybe the rental guy will come looking for his boats. He might send out the coastguard, or maybe someone else will come and we can get them to take us away."

"But when will he come? Maybe he doesn't care and won't bother looking. He was flaky, and hardly even interested in renting the boats," said Carl.

"True, but he'll want them back. When we don't show, he'll come. Why wouldn't he?"

"Because we have the boats?" suggested Izzy.

"If he doesn't have his own, he'll get someone to bring him to see what's going on. It's not very far at all, so I'm sure he'll be here later this evening at the latest."

"I really hope so," said Carl. "I hate this place, and this is the most talking I've done in years. I like to be alone, not stuck with strangers on a murderous island full of crazies."

"I'm with you there," I chuckled, wringing out my dripping hair.

"Let's get you dried," said Izzy. "There's plenty of towels at the cafe, and it's still sunny and warm enough for your boxers to dry out if you just sit out, or we can hang them up. Babs, Bob, are you both able to walk?"

"Of course we are," said Babs. "The water sobered us up more than we'd like, so let's go." Seemingly fine now, she sprang to her feet, Bob did likewise, so we marched back towards the cafe, dripping as we went, but at least it was sunny and if nothing else we knew exactly where we stood now.

The killer was definitely out to get us, and was upping his or her game. The fun was over. This was now about as serious as it got, and we were in the firing line.

Anxious behaved impeccably now the excitement was over, and stayed close as we retraced our steps yet again back to the cafe, passing the row of cottages but not knocking on any more doors as we were exhausted, confused, and yes, scared of who or what we might encounter.

We needed to rest, and we needed to get dry, so while Izzy went inside to see what she could find, the rest of us took a seat at the one table and waited. When Izzy returned with towels and even some pegs she'd found, Bob and Babs stripped down coyly then wrapped themselves up before hanging their clothes out to dry. With the sun and the breeze, it shouldn't take too long, but I felt strangely exposed sitting in my boxer shorts with a murderer on the loose. At least I had my Crocs, so that was something, and I smiled smugly as they were already dry. Yay for Crocs!

"Max, why are you looking so relaxed?" asked Izzy as she scooted her chair over beside mine. The others turned to me, strangely interested.

"Because my feet are dry, I'm alive, and so are the rest of you. That's a good thing."

"It's not just that, is it? There's something else. And I wouldn't get too smug. Your feet may be dry, but your footwear is a crime against fashion. Didn't anyone tell you that you aren't allowed to wear Crocs out in public? They're for in the garden or at campsites." Izzy winked, but I knew she wasn't really joking.

"I don't care! They make me happy, and it isn't doing any harm. Since I became a vanlifer, I've learned so much about the world and even more about myself. For the first time ever, I don't care what people think. No, let me rephrase that. Of course I care, but I don't let it affect me. I can wear Crocs if I want. I can live an unconventional life. Living how I do means I get to see all sorts of people doing things a little differently, and it's a real eye-opener. Not everyone conforms, and that's awesome. Fashion is fleeting, and years from now I'm sure everything we are currently wearing will be seen as ridiculous. Not so long ago men wore tights."

"Bob still does on our special nights," tittered Babs.

"Ssh, that's private," said Bob, reddening.

"Anyway, what I mean is, just because people think differently doesn't mean they're right. I've finally learned to let go and not get so stressed about the little things. Even the big things. Everything will work out here, you mark my words. It may seem like all is lost, but it isn't. Life has a way of working out."

"Tell that to the dead dudes," said Carl.

"Hey, stop putting a downer on things," said Izzy. "Max, I think that's beautiful. I wish I could live a life like yours. Isn't it lonely? Don't you miss a proper home?"

"Sometimes it's lonely, but isn't everyone? The bigger the city, the more isolated people seem to be. As to a proper home? Sometimes I miss it. But every morning I wake up and step outside I feel connected to the world like I never did before. It's a beautiful thing. I'm free, and won't ever go back to my old life."

"Now I really am jealous," she laughed, smiling at me.

"No need to be. You can do what you want with your life. If you're serious enough about something, you'll find a way to make it a reality. It took my entire life collapsing around me, and from my own doing, for me to get the wake-up call and finally change things. Now I roam, and I couldn't be happier. Plus, I have this guy to keep me company, so I'm never truly alone."

"Sounds idyllic," said Bob, "but wait until the winter then see if you feel the same way."

"I'm not worried. I'm looking forward to the challenge, and to see how I cope. I know I will. I know this sounds dumb, but I love my van. I called her Vee, which isn't very imaginative for a VW campervan, but she's like family. I really miss her."

"Miss a vehicle!" scoffed Bob. "You're crazy."

"I don't think you are," said Carl. "I spend too much time on the road with the band, and although we aren't exactly vanlifers we do spend weeks away from home. It's a different world out there when you travel a lot, and it's exciting, but man is it exhausting. Without the deadlines to play gigs and having to sleep in crappy hotels because there's not enough room for everyone in the van, I think it would be incredible. Good for you, Max."

"Thanks. I appreciate that. Now, how about I make us something for dinner? Anyone hungry?"

Everyone was famished, so I wrapped a towel around my waist then went into the cafe to see what I could rustle up.

Chapter 10

Although the cafe had a commercial kitchen of sorts, it was beyond basic. As the menu suggested, things weren't set up for mass catering, or much in the way of food at all. This was a tea and scones type of place, and I discovered that the scones weren't even fresh but were frozen. In the large chest freezer I did uncover a few choice ingredients, but you can't cook with frozen meat so I was even more limited.

The large fridge held a surprising array of fresh ingredients, however, and I was pleasantly surprised by what I discovered. The cupboards were also well-stocked, and I could only assume that Pink was quite a foodie but didn't care to share his culinary skills with tourists, but must have used the kitchen on a daily basis for his own cooking. He must have made a shopping trip to the mainland recently as everything was still in date, and I became excited about the chance to do what I loved doing best.

The circumstances may have been dire, and to say I was in the right frame of mind to cook would be a lie, but I knew that once I got going my cares would slip away and I'd feel better; I was right.

With a pan sizzling, I was determined to stick to my one-pot ethos, no matter that I was cooking for five people and one famished, forlorn dog, so chose my ingredients with care, and even went so far as to cook Anxious' dinner separately so he didn't get onions and a few other things I'd learned dogs weren't supposed to eat.

The fridge was a fisherman's paradise, and I chose some bass so fresh I worried it would start flapping about—it couldn't have been more than a day old. It smelled of nothing, always a good sign when it came to fish, so bass it would be for dinner.

I started with a dough, and with the heat rising as the oven warmed it soon rose, so once the bass and everything else was good to go, I let a pot simmer with a plethora of fresh veg and some cans of beans then formed my flatbreads, let them rest as dinner would be a while, then went to relax until it was time to cook them and add the pan-fried fish back into the pot.

Back out in the cafe, everyone was trying their best to relax, which was easier said than done after what we'd been through this afternoon. Stress levels were high, we were concerned about how far the killer had gone to to ensure nobody got off the island, and nobody knew what to do.

Anxious was exhausted and even though I'd told him he could hang with me in the kitchen he'd simply curled up by the door and fallen asleep. I knew that if it opened he'd be alert in a flash, so I left him to rest while I joined the others.

"What's the plan?" asked Izzy as I sat.

"The plan?"

"Yeah, Max, what now?" asked Bob.

"Should we try to find the other residents, or wait it out until morning and hope that someone comes to rescue us?" asked Carl.

Everyone leaned forward and waited for me to answer, and I was taken aback. "Why are you all asking me what to do? Haven't you been talking about it while I was in the kitchen?"

"We've been talking, but nobody has come up with anything useful," said Carl. "We decided we'd wait for our leader and see what he had to say."

"And you've chosen me as the leader?"

The group looked confused, and exchanged glances with one another, then Carl said, "We didn't choose you. It's just the way it is, isn't it? I mean, you're the, you know, the…"

"The one in charge," said Bob, nodding his head at the others who agreed.

"Yeah, the one in charge. Max, you knew that, right? You've been leading us ever since you came to find us at the castle. You've told us what to do, explained what happened, and tried to fix this. Not that you can fix the dead guys, obviously, but you are in charge."

"You're the alpha," said Babs. "Not that my Bob isn't manly and strong and the absolute best, but some people are born to lead and others are born to do other things."

"I never thought of myself like that. I guess my time in commercial kitchens has made me quite good at giving orders, but I'm sorry if I've been bossy."

"Mate, you haven't been bossy. You've handled the situation well, if you ask me, and trust me, I don't normally give compliments." Carl slapped me on the back and laughed, clearly as uncomfortable as me with the way this had gone. "You're in charge as you acted like you were from the get-go. Nobody's saying you weren't polite and you haven't been bossy or anything, and we appreciate you looking out for us. Some people would have tried to leave and left us behind, but you didn't. You care. That's awesome."

The others spoke words of encouragement and I found it both a confidence booster and rather concerning. Carl was right in that I had been concerned for everyone's safety, but it was a lot of pressure to know that these people saw me as the one who would keep them safe. I had absolutely no idea how to do that, but would do my best and hopefully come the morning we could leave this place and never, ever return.

"So, what's the plan?" asked Izzy.

"If it was just me, I'd lock the door, eat my dinner, get some sleep, then in the morning try to find the other residents, see what they have to say and if they can help, and hopefully someone will arrive to get us. There are people waiting for me, so they'll be worried by now, and maybe that's the same for some of you?" I enquired.

"Nobody is waiting for me," lamented Izzy. "I'm here on my own and camping not far away. I hate travelling solo, but I've done it for so long I suppose I'm used to it now."

"Sorry to hear that," said Carl, smiling warmly at Izzy who blushed a little and smiled back. "I'm the same. Like I said, I spend a lot of time on the road with the band, so like to do my own thing when I get the chance. I've been travelling about for a few weeks, camping like Izzy, and just seeing the sights and relaxing."

"And we have our caravan," said Babs. "We come to Cornwall every year. It's our main holiday. We've never been here before though."

"And we won't be coming back," said Bob.

I couldn't help it, but I burst out laughing as I said, "I don't think I will either."

The others joined me, and soon the cafe was filled with the sounds of our laughter as we joked about ever returning to such a terrible place. Once our mirth subsided we seemed to have formed a tight bond in our little group, first impressions forgotten as we got used to one another's ways and Carl ditched his moody expressions and curt, short sentences and began to act like part of the team.

A team I was somehow in charge of.

With the ice well and truly broken everyone seemed to get a second wind, so despite the intensity of the situation and the heightened stress levels, we fell into an easy banter as everyone helped to prepare for dinner in our little oasis of calm when outside who knew what madness raged.

Babs and Bob were in charge of drinks, and even paid for them for everyone, and poured wine whilst having a few extra cheeky ones themselves. Carl and Izzy set the table, placing crockery and cutlery, while I escaped to the kitchen and put the finishing touches to the dish and let the fish warm through in the strong sauce that had been bubbling for an hour now.

Satisfied, and with a final taste test then a quick addition of extra seasoning, the dish was ready. The flatbreads cooked to perfection in minutes, and I knew that with some melted butter they'd be a true joy. Carefully, I carried the entire large pot out into the cafe and placed it in the centre of the table to a generous round of applause. I hurried to retrieve the bread and butter, then set the plate down, my mouth watering.

"Anything wrong?" I asked as the room become strangely silent. "It doesn't look that bad, does it? It's been a rush, and I didn't have all the ingredients I'd have liked, but the flatbreads are fresh even though it would have been nice to make a proper loaf if we had a few more hours, and the fish should be decent."

The others looked at each other, then to me, and clapped again.

Anxious came over, woken by the noise, then sat and waited for about a millisecond before barking and jumping up to try to see what was on the table.

"Ah, almost forget. Anxious, here's yours. I made it special so there are no onions or garlic, but you'll like the fish and there are some lovely soft potatoes in the stew."

The finer points were lost on my best buddy as I placed a bowl down for him. Ravenous, he tucked straight in, while I raised an eyebrow at the others and waited nervously for someone to say something.

"How did you do that?" asked Izzy, eyeing the meal greedily.

"What do you mean? It's alright isn't it? Why is everyone acting so strangely? I know we're under a lot of stress, but I thought this might help."

"Max, we're just stunned you managed to cook something that looks so amazing, smells incredible, and I'm sure will taste fabulous," said Babs with a shake of her head as if the simple meal was the best thing she'd seen in her life.

"We expected really basic grub, not this. It looks fit for a king," gushed Bob.

"Very impressive," agreed Carl.

"Phew. You had me worried there for a moment." I picked up the ladle then dished up a generous portion and a well-buttered flatbread after checking everyone wanted one. Once they'd been served, I took my seat and said, "Let's eat!"

We clinked glasses, the mood buoyant, then tucked in. Anxious was already finished, so had extra bread then returned to the door and kept guard. He was asleep in under a minute!

During dinner, we chatted about this and that, learning a little more about each other. We tried to keep things as light as possible, although it was a struggle because the stress hadn't gone, just receded whilst we were cocooned in our own intimate world, well aware that things could change at any moment.

Bob and Babs were happily married and had been for decades. Having taken part-time early retirement, they travelled as often as they could but were also immensely proud of their home and garden, and when not off on an adventure in their caravan spent most of their time outside at home tending to the plants and drinking copious amounts of wine, which they freely admitted. Their jobs as morticians were still important, but they had cut their work to a few hours a week and had decided that this would be their last year before they retired completely.

Carl was more reticent to talk about himself, but I gathered that he spent a lot of time with his band and lived alone, but also enjoyed making the most of the country and adored camping solo. He admitted that he wasn't always the easiest person to get along with, and was often moody and liked to keep to himself, but he showed his other side this evening and was even fun on occasion.

Izzy was somewhat of a dark horse, and I was intrigued by her. She apologised again for the impromptu mime, but explained that it was almost impossible to resist performing once the subject arose even though she, and all other mime artists on the planet, knew that it made most people extremely uncomfortable.

"It's the faces," she sighed. "I don't know why, but we're all the same. The moment we begin our act we find ourselves pulling these crazy expressions. It's part of the show, you see. We have to show emotion somehow, so we exaggerate our features. It makes people feel uncomfortable, especially if we get close to them when we're escaping from our invisible boxes or climbing out of pretend windows. I honestly don't know what comes over me. It's almost like an out-of-body experience. I come back to myself at the end of a show and don't even remember what I've done."

"And people pay you to perform?" asked Carl dubiously.

"They do. It's a crazy thing. I never thought I'd ever become a mime artist, even though I always had an interest in it and got taught by some of the greatest in the country. I got a job years ago performing for an elderly couple. They booked me as they'd seen me performing in the street. I used to be a busker. It took off from there and I've never looked back. Now I get paid really good money to do my act for wealthy people at functions and it always goes down a storm."

"No offence, Izzy, but I didn't realise there were so many fans. How come they want a mime artist at their functions?" I asked, genuinely intrigued.

"Beats me!" she laughed.

We finished dinner, and everyone congratulated me on the meal, which I was pleased about. It may have been a simple enough dish, but as always I tried to do my very best and no matter how many meals you cook for others, you always enjoy it when they show appreciation.

I insisted on cleaning up, and after Babs helped clear the table and put things in the kitchen I shooed her back into the cafe while I merrily washed and dried up then cleaned down the counters, wiped over the gas hob, and even gave the oven door a thorough scrub too.

Standing back, I admired my handiwork and felt a true sense of satisfaction. I'd always been like this, even when I worked in expensive restaurants, and ensured the kitchen was spotless at the end of each shift and would usually go over things myself even though there were others who cleaned. It was part of the ritual, and an important one, as there was nothing worse than going to work to prep for the day only to discover that the kitchen wasn't as it should be. Using someone else's kitchen, even if Pink was now dead, meant it was doubly important to leave it as good as, if not better than, when I'd found it.

Back in the cafe, the others were sitting around and chatting quietly as they drank their wine, and I sank into my chair gratefully and took the offered glass from Babs.

"Drink up. It's going to be a long night and it will help you to relax."

"Thanks, Babs." The wine was cold and fruity and I savoured it now that the meal was over and I'd finished my chores, so settled back and enjoyed the buzz as the room slowly quietened as everyone was lost to their own thoughts.

Anxious whimpered in his sleep, and I worried for him being away from Vee. Ever since we'd embarked on this new life he'd slept either in Vee or in a tent with me, but the van was where we loved to be. Now we were far away from her, miles out of our comfort zone, and surrounded by strangers on an island where a murderer was on the loose and we had no idea who it was or how we might escape.

As the evening wore on, Bob and Babs became rather animated as they drank more than the rest of us and seemingly could go on the whole night. I was exhausted, though, and Izzy and Carl looked the same, so we hunted around until we found some blankets and cleared a space in the cafe so we could bed down and rest.

Nobody wanted privacy, everyone wanted to stay together, so we laid out the blankets to make one huge bed then took turns using the bathroom, which everyone was beyond pleased to have as nobody wanted to venture outside, then we lay down and had no choice but to huddle up.

It felt odd to be sleeping with strangers, and judging by the nervous coughs and apologies as we shifted about to get comfortable, everyone felt the same. It was only when Babs began to laugh, which was contagious and we admitted how we felt, that we relaxed.

With the light left on, and with Anxious having somehow ninja-slid across the floor then up under the covers from the bottom only to pop up beside me, grinning, I cuddled him and tried to get some sleep.

Chapter 11

"Is everyone asleep?" asked Izzy after we'd been lying there for all of no minutes.

"Nope," said Carl.

"We're not going to sleep tonight," said Babs. "We decided to lie down because you all wanted to, but we agreed there is no way we're shutting our eyes when there's a maniac on the loose. That woman freaked us out earlier too. Green is a witch and she might be outside the door casting a spell, ready to carve our chests."

"That's right," agreed Bob. "My Babs and I are going to stay awake and listen for intruders. Do we have weapons?"

"Just the oars," said Carl. "Although there is a kitchen full of knives. Maybe we should all have one just in case."

"I'm not sure that's a good idea. Unless any of you know how to knife fight, it might end up being more dangerous than not having one."

"But you've got one under your bag," protested Babs. "I saw you put it there."

"Babs, that's different. Max is our leader and in charge of keeping us safe, so of course he's got a knife."

"I think I should have one too," said Carl, sitting up.

"Can you please stop calling me the leader and saying I'll protect you?" I asked. "It's a lot of pressure and I'm not sure I'm comfortable with the responsibility."

"Come on, Max. Let's get real here." Carl turned to me, so I sat up and listened to what he had to say. "I may not know you very well, but I do know that ever since you met us you've been thinking about how you can protect everyone. You've been worried about the gang's safety, have looked out for us, and are the one who makes the decisions. So you are our leader. The sign that you're a true leader is that you don't want to be. They should do the same for the prime minister. If anyone wants to do that job, they clearly have a screw loose and are an utter megalomaniac. It should only be given to someone who doesn't want to do it. They couldn't do a worse job."

"He's got a point," said Bob. "About you and the PM. Maybe Max should be prime minister?"

"I would absolutely refuse," I laughed. "I want to live in my van with Anxious and wait for Min to agree to join us."

"You love her very much, don't you?" asked Babs, smiling in sympathy.

"More than anything. I hope she isn't too worried. My parents will be waiting by now too. They were coming this evening and will have met up with Min. I bet they'll be going spare."

"That's so sweet. I'm sure Min will join you in your new life soon enough. By the sounds of it, you guys spend plenty of time together anyway."

"We sure do, and I love it. But we're taking it slowly to ensure it's the right decision. It is, but the wait will mean we'll appreciate it all the more when we finally get back together."

"You sound pretty confident that you will," said Carl. "If you're both so certain, how come you haven't got back together permanently already?"

"Like I told everyone earlier, I screwed up in a spectacular way. I don't blame her for waiting to ensure I don't revert to my old ways. She knows by now that won't happen, but I understand. It was my fault, and she'll never risk being hurt again. And besides, it's kind of romantic."

"It really is," gushed Babs. "Soul mates torn apart by one man's obsession, only to be re-united over the love of the open road and endless murder mysteries! So sweet."

"I could do without quite as many murders," I admitted. "Especially when I'm stuck on an island with the killer."

"Let's get up and go for a walk," said Izzy. "I'm going stir-crazy in here and there's no way I'll ever sleep. Maybe we should go to the harbour, not that we even need to walk anywhere, and see if there's anyone about. It's not even very late. It's only ten. There might be boats. We could signal to them."

"With what?" scoffed Carl.

"Dunno. A fire? Shout? I need to do something. I'm beyond stressed and scared. So scared. Anyone?"

"I'll come. Anxious hasn't been out for a pee yet. But we have to stick together, and never go off alone. Agreed."

"Yes, leader," said Izzy, grinning as she teased me.

The others were loathe to remain inside without us, so after a bit of huffing and puffing, and everyone looking the other way as for some inexplicable reason Bob had stripped down to his birthday suit even though he'd been wedged between me and Babs, we gathered at the door.

Anxious sat facing us with his head cocked, curious why we were so reticent to go out on our nighttime adventure.

"There is a bad man out there," I explained.

"Or woman," offered Izzy brightly.

"Yes, or woman."

"Or two men, or two women, or a man and a woman," added Bob with a chuckle.

"Yes, any combination, or a sole killer," I sighed. "Anxious, you must stay close, you must stay alert, and you must protect us. Agreed?"

A bark in the affirmative and a glance at my pocket meant he understood, so with a treat to encourage him, I unlocked the door and flung it open, not sure what I was expecting, but it wasn't anything good.

A communal sigh of relief escaped our lips when the coast was clear. With the light of the cafe to guide us, we locked up then slowly walked past the cottages towards the jetty. No lights shone outside the houses, and the curtains stopped any light from inside escaping, if anyone was still up, but the illumination at the jetty meant the area was bathed in an orange glow that made the going easy.

We stood at the jetty and looked out to sea, but there was nothing but the moon peeking cautiously from behind a stubborn cloud. We waited for at least ten minutes, silent and apprehensive, then we noticed the light at the same time. Then another, and another.

"They've come to rescue us!" cheered Babs, hugging Bob.

"Maybe. Let's wait and see," I said. "The boats are a long way off, and I can't even tell if they're heading our way or not. Nobody get their hopes up too much."

We waited, eyes locked on the bobbing lights that sometimes seemed to get closer, other times vanished altogether. I wondered what the fishermen were after, as I assumed they were fishing, and eventually we had to admit that they were not coming to rescue us and didn't even know we were here.

Eventually, we gave up, and I suggested that maybe we should move the bodies while it was cool, as tomorrow they would be in a terrible state if they were out in the sun all day. Izzy and Carl were reluctant, Bob and Babs had zero qualms about manhandling corpses as they did it regularly, so guided by the torches on our phones we skirted the coast of the island until we found the man who'd been tied up like a scarecrow.

He was still where we'd left him, and a rather gruesome sight by torchlight, but between us we managed to rig up a simple stretcher after Bob showed us how, and carried him back to the cafe then into the rear storage room. Exhausted, but knowing this was far from over, we gathered some things, including a tarpaulin after we agreed that old Pink was way too heavy to carry far, then headed back out again.

After manhandling Pink onto the tarp, we dragged him back to the cafe and lay him carefully beside the other man. We checked the mystery man for any ID again, but came up with nothing once more, which I think unnerved me more than anything else. Who was he? Where did he come from? How long had he been on the island, and why had nobody come to look for him? The mysteries just kept piling up.

"Now what are we meant to do?" asked Carl.

"No way can I sleep with these guys in the building." Izzy shuddered.

"They can't harm you," said Bob. "They're dead and at peace. Nothing to fear from the deceased."

"I know that from a logical point of view, but they've both got weird symbols carved into their flesh by an utter maniac, so it's tough to chill out and relax. Can we go back outside? Maybe have a wander?" Izzy glanced at the door as if she was about to make a run for it.

"Is that smart in the dark?" asked Bob. "We're safer inside with the door locked."

"No way am I staying in here," grumbled Carl.

"Me either," said Izzy. "It's creeping me right out. I want to go outside. Even sitting by the jetty with a blanket is preferable. I want out. I think I might be having a panic attack." Izzy had turned very pale, which was saying something as her red hair and fair complexion meant she would never tan much, and her hands were shaking.

Babs took her to one side and they spoke quietly for a while until her nerves settled, then Babs asked, "Is it alright if we all go back outside? I know bringing the men inside was the right thing to do, but it isn't fair on those who aren't used to seeing death."

"Sure, if that's what everyone wants?" I asked.

They did, and right now, so we grabbed a few things, meaning wine and blankets—guess who grabbed what?—then locked up again and returned to the quiet of the jetty.

We sat on the surprisingly warm planks, close to one another for the comfort it brought rather than the warmth, and once again watched the fishing boats bobbing on the water. I thanked Bob when he handed me a small bottle of wine, and drank it slowly, enjoying the warmth it brought and the relaxation as the night wore on, one long minute after another.

Anxious curled up on my lap and snored, content and unafraid, and I envied him such peace of mind. I even began to hear things, and was certain I heard Mum and Dad bickering far out to sea, which brought a smile to my face. I could picture them now, Dad rowing around and around in circles, both of them missing the island by several miles and ending up who knew where. With their lack of map reading skills and utter absence of any sense of direction, they'd most likely end up in France if they had tried to rescue me. Once landed, they'd start talking very loudly and slowly so they could be understood, which was how they both always acted around anyone foreign or even northerners.

Their arguing faded as the wind picked up, carrying my daydreams with it, replaced with the cry of an occasional gull, but apart from that all was silent.

Then something else caught my attention, and this time I knew I wasn't imagining it.

"Listen," I whispered. "Can you hear that?"

Everyone turned to the cottages where I pointed, and remained silent until the noise happened again. It was a simple clang, like metal hitting metal, followed by a dull thud. What could it be? Should we try to find out? I stood, cradling Anxious, to better hear, and the others joined me. As if in a trance, we were drawn by the sound and shuffled towards it, but I suddenly stopped and asked, "Does everyone feel alright? I'm not sure I do. I was just imagining voices of my parents and now I'm sure my head's messed up."

"That'll be the wine," said Babs merrily, swigging from her bottle.

"I don't think so. It's something else. Of course!" I gasped. "I used the water to rinse out the fish and a little for stock as well as the wine I reduced. The note said not to drink the water. Maybe boiling it stopped it being so dangerous, but what if it's done something to us? How is everyone feeling?"

"I feel kind of trippy," murmured Carl as if from far away. "I'm not out of it or anything, but my body is tingly and I'm lightheaded. Like I'm walking on a cloud. It's not as bad as it was, and to be honest I put it down to the wine and the stress. But, yeah, I'm not quite right."

"Izzy?"

"Nothing like that. Just a slightly strange sensation all over. Like very mild pins and needles. I can think straight, but my head is fuzzy."

"I feel great!" laughed Babs.

"But do you think you should, given the circumstances?" I asked.

"Maybe not," she admitted. "But I'm gonna go with it as the other option is to be terrified."

Bob coughed to clear his throat, then cuddled Babs before offering his insights. "I have to admit, I assumed it was the wine, too, but there is something else going on. Like Izzy, I have faint pins and needles and my thoughts are a little wild. I swear I heard voices not so long ago. For a moment I pictured mermaids," he giggled.

"So we're agreed that even without the wine, we wouldn't be feeling a hundred percent. Of course, our stress levels are heightened, but the way I feel now is like yesterday when I was drugged. Very mild, but it's there. I can focus, but it's an effort, and although not unpleasant, it is very disconcerting. I don't like to think that something's been done to us without our knowledge or consent. But how can it be in the water? I did wonder about this yesterday, but where does the water actually come from? Do they get it delivered? That would be a massive undertaking."

"What could they put in the water?" asked Carl. "And how could they do it? What's the point?"

"My guess is that whoever killed the others poisoned the water so they could kill them. I don't know what it is, but if it knocked me out, it would have done the same to them. I think we need to go and see what the noise is as the locals might be in trouble. I know it's a risk and I'm not asking anyone to come with me. Anxious and I can investigate and report back, but even though they were odd, I wouldn't want anyone I'd met to be next on the killers list."

"I'm coming too." Carl locked his gaze on mine and nodded. He was determined, and I wouldn't try to change his mind.

"What if they try to hurt us?" squealed Babs, wrapping her arms around Bob and sobbing into his chest, the tension finally getting too much for her.

"Bob, maybe you should take Babs back to the cafe and lock yourselves inside? You'll be safe then. We won't be long, and I was going to suggest that only a few of us go as that way we'll be less likely to get caught. Can you do that? Here are the keys."

"Sure, Max. And thanks. I see what you're doing, and I appreciate it. Come on, love, let's get you tucked under the blankets and maybe a nice cold glass of wine to calm your nerves. How does that sound?"

"Perfect," she murmured, righting herself and dabbing at her eyes as she smiled wanly at me. "Thank you, Max. Thank you everyone. You're so kind and I've tried to be brave, but dealing with this has been too much. I'd much rather handle dead bodies than fear for my life." She giggled nervously, then let Bob lead her towards the cafe. I watched as they went inside, then the door closed.

"She'll be fine," said Carl almost casually, before rubbing vigorously at his scalp and grimacing. "Man, I don't like this feeling. I am so close to freaking out and tearing at my skin, but I think it's fading now. How long do you think it lasts?"

"I'm feeling a lot better already," I assured him. "My best guess is that you get the full effects in less than an hour, then it begins to fade soon after. It's hard to know as I'm so out of sorts anyway, but this is more like how I felt once I came around after being unconscious. Let this be a warning for everyone. No drinking any water unless it's from a sealed bottle."

"I'm sticking to wine just to be sure," laughed Izzy, taking a generous swig and finishing her miniature bottle.

"Good idea," agreed Carl, gulping his.

Deciding I needed a little fortification, too, I drank mine then we wandered over to the collection of bins and popped the empties in the recycling one, careful to make no noise, then I closed the lid and we stood around, eyeing the cottages nervously, the sound continuing, beating a rhythm that got into my bones.

"What is that noise?" asked Carl.

"Time to find out."

Chapter 12

The simple row of five brightly coloured fisherman's cottages were undoubtedly quaint, but now, at just gone midnight, they were eerie. Whereas during the day, with the sun shining on the roofs and bouncing off the crisp paintwork, they were picture-postcard perfect, the less than favourable light from the cafe and jetty revealed their true state.

The paintwork was less than pristine, with numerous deep pockets in shadow where the gaps between stone hadn't been reached. The windows were partially rotten, especially the upper storeys, and the roof slates were in desperate need of replacing. Weeds sprung from the wonky chimneys, and although this gave them a charming appeal on first arriving, now they just looked sinister and poorly maintained.

"How do we get to the back?" asked Izzy, gripping my arm then grabbing Carl's and pulling him in close to us.

"There's no way in from by the cafe, but on this side there's a fence and I think there might be a gate. Let's take a look. I think they access whatever's there via their back doors. Both White and Green were insistent that nobody went out there, but there's definitely something going on."

With our arms linked, we approached the simple, high wooden fence that ran from the wall to the rock face behind the houses. It wasn't very long, but it would afford at least some private outdoor space. No more than five paces, it would just about fit a small table and chairs, possibly a few plant pots, but not much more. Although, I had seen numerous miraculous small gardens on the TV over the years, so maybe it was a gardeners' paradise the other side of the sun-bleached panel fence.

"There's no gate," lamented Izzy as we inspected the half-rotten structure.

"Are you sure?" asked Carl with a wink. He unlinked his arm from Izzy then grabbed a plank and yanked.

Izzy gasped as he repeated it for another board, then slipped through and beckoned us to follow.

"This is seeming like a terrible idea," I groaned, wincing as Carl rapped on the fence to tell us to hurry up.

"We need to find out what's making the noise. What if someone's in danger?" Izzy was resolute, and before I could stop her she squeezed through then crooked her index finger for me to follow.

"What do you think, Anxious?" I asked, bending to stroke his head.

He looked from me to the fence, then licked my hand before darting through then poking his head back out and grinning.

"Guess I have my answer," I chuckled, my nerves rising. Maybe it was the need to uncover the truth, the worry harm was coming to someone else, or possibly the poisoned water addling my brain, but I followed then stood stock still and waited for my eyes to adjust to the lower light levels.

We were in the rear courtyard of the blue house, and it wasn't at all what I had expected. A light shone from above the low UPVC back door, casting a rather friendly glow over the neat yard. For such a small space, it felt much larger than it was thanks to smart planning and the plethora of plants. Ferns and hostas in pots gave it a tropical feel, while large fuchsia bushes cheered up the space with their low hanging bursts of red, white, and purple.

Most of the space was taken up by a cast-iron round table and two chairs, with a single glass beside a half-finished bottle of Pinot. A bottle of water was open and half drunk, strangely without any label whatsoever.

But all of this was taken in with little more than a glance, because the real focal point was the looming entrance to a cave. Protected by the high fence from the harbour side, it was only five feet or so at the mouth but seemed to spread along the length of the houses.

We crept forward to the end of the fence between the garden and next door, noting that the same fencing was repeated for each yard. The panels stopped just before the cave entrance at each property, meaning they all had access not only to each other's gardens if they so wished, but to the cave as well.

"This is freaky, man. I don't like this one bit. What's the noise in the cave? What are they doing in there?"

"I have no idea, and I'm not sure it's a good idea to find out. Whatever it is, they're doing all they can to keep it private. There's no mention of it on the tourist leaflet, and nobody else has said a word about it. I don't think anyone knows it exists. We should leave."

"Agreed," said Carl.

"It's creeping me out," said Izzy with a shudder as she turned to slip through the fence.

At that moment, Anxious decided that he knew best, and after glancing at me he ran between Izzy's legs then into the cave and was lost to darkness.

"Anxious!" I hissed, but I knew he couldn't hear me and I didn't want to raise my voice as what kind of trouble would we be in then? Without him, I felt exposed and vulnerable, as though part of me was missing, and I instantly worried for his safety.

"I thought he was a good dog?" asked Izzy.

"He is. He's the best. Something must have made him do it. Maybe he smelled something. I'll have to go and get him. You can both wait here if you want."

"No way!" they both whispered.

With a nod, I led the way, only pausing briefly at the cave's entrance before forging ahead, the way lit by a single string of warm white bulbs making it feel like I was entering fairyland or a Christmas grotto.

If I met Santa I was going to utterly freak out!

After a handful of seconds, my eyes had adjusted enough to make out the interior, but there wasn't much to see beyond rock and more rock. We eased forward cautiously, careful not to make a sound, and followed the lights down a gradient so soon enough we were able to stand upright as the cave easily tripled in height until the roof was lost to shadow.

As the entrance receded behind us and I grew concerned just how far we'd have to run if we had to make a speedy exit, the clattering and rhythmic banging grew in intensity until it got into my bones. I got the strange feeling I was about to enter a drum 'n' bass late night club and we'd turn a corner and find hundreds of people bouncing to the beats.

But as we did turn the corner, there were no pulsing lights, or DJs, or pounding speakers, just a relatively compact cave that went no further. Lights were strung up criss-crossing the modest space, casting sharp shadows on the rough, curved walls, and joy of joys, Anxious was sitting not five feet from us, head cocked, watching proceedings with a concerned occasional wag of his tail. His ears were down, and yet he must have sensed my presence because he turned just after we arrived, then ran back over and pawed at my legs insistently.

I crouched and scooped him up then gave him a massive hug, as much to lessen my own growing sense of unease as to comfort the little guy.

"You shouldn't run off like that," I whispered into his now pert ear.

Anxious wagged happily, then licked my chin.

"What are they doing?" asked Carl, his voice so quiet it took me a moment to decipher the words.

"I have no idea, but I'm not sure we want to find out. It's like some weird cult thing."

"I'm not so sure, although Green is certainly making a spectacle."

"Guys, this is freaking me out," gasped Izzy as she wiped her brow and her eyes roamed.

"Me too," I admitted, the fight-or-flight impulses growing by the second, the flight response far greater than the fight one.

"Then let's go," said Carl. "We've seen enough."

"Just give me one moment. I want to make sense of this."

Both nodded uneasily, so we kept close and tried to control our breathing as we watched the strange spectacle unfolding before us. In truth, there wasn't much to see. All five residents, and it was easy to know they were the genuine ones because each was dressed head-to-toe in the colour of their houses, plus I'd already met three of them, were stood in a loose semi-circle facing what I believed to be a simple well pump. One of the manual ones where you had to work a lever. This machine was slightly different to any I'd ever seen on the TV or the few I'd seen in reality, as it seemed to have not only a tap but attached to the base was a thick hose that wound off across the ground a ways before burrowing like an oversized worm.

The brother of the deceased Pink, the new Pink, was pumping the handle vigorously, and each time he did the machine squealed and the rhythm pulsed. His huge frame dwarfed the handle, his thick arms engorged and beefy with veins even though he carried a lot of extra weight. His pink vest and salmon shorts that were way too small for him made him look comical in one regard, and an utterly menacing maniac in all others.

With a nod to the others, he ceased his work, took a massive drink from the tap, then stepped back. Green, who wore the same clothes as yesterday, stopped what she was doing—which was chanting with her eyes closed and waving a crystal overhead—then opened her eyes and nodded in return to Pink before taking up the mantle and pumping the handle.

Their difference in size was almost comical, and she had to work very hard to get it going, but once she did she got into a rhythm and for the next few minutes we watched in awe as she built up a sweat as she pumped water to who knew where. Once she was finished, she repeated Pink's actions and bent to the tap, turned the little wheel, and as the water gushed into a gully she drank heartily, not stopping until she must have drunk litres of the stuff.

As she stepped away, I noticed that those who had already had their turn, namely Blue, Pink, and now Green, seemed to fall into a trance. They swayed to the rhythm as White took his turn, hands raised above their heads, eyes closed in rapture as they craned their necks towards the roof of the cave.

Green finished soon enough, so White took over. It gave me the chance to study the other residents, and I was shocked by Red's appearance the most. Whereas Blue was a rather nondescript diminutive man of between sixty and seventy with a wiry frame like Green's, with white hair and simple blue jeans and a blue vest, Red was an altogether more flamboyant character.

As she took her place after White finished, I couldn't stop looking at this strange woman. She was tall, easily six three, with a regal elegance and a profile to match. Rather square jaw, with a sharp nose that'd been broken and reset badly, it made her entire face seem somehow off. Maybe it was the thin, determined and pursed lips, or the receding jaw or large teeth, but it was as though the separate features didn't quite meld together, like they belonged to different people. Her attire was even more arresting.

A bright red beret covered equally as shocking hair, with matching lipstick. She wore a full ballgown, as dark as congealed blood, with a pair of red socks but no shoes. The gown glittered as the lights caught the sequins and the string of pearls around her neck, her pale skin slightly flushed as she worked the pump, slender arms criss-crossed with veins as she worked hard.

"We need to go," I finally told the others, coming out of the trance. "They'll be done soon and then they might leave. Come on." Cradling Anxious, I turned and retraced our steps, the others beside me. Nobody said a word.

As the rhythms receded and the cave entrance appeared as we made the turn, we each exhaled sharply, relief washing over us. We hurried to the courtyard, slipped through the fence, then Carl replaced the planks and we dashed away like trippy ninjas towards the cafe, only pausing once we were outside it. I performed the secret knock we'd agreed on earlier to let Babs and Bob know we were here. I waited, then raised an eyebrow to the others when nobody came, so knocked again, this time as loudly as I dared.

Thankfully, footsteps clattered across the floor and a timid voice asked, "Who's there?"

"It's us."

"Us who?" asked Bob.

"Max, Izzy, Carl, and Anxious."

"How do I know it's really you? You might be trying to trick me. You could be anyone."

"We had a secret knock, remember?" I hissed, exasperated and concerned we might be seen once the others finished in the cave.

"But if you captured our friends you might have tortured them until they told you about the secret knock. Prove it."

Anxious barked, then whined as he scratched at the door.

"Anxious!" shouted Bob, then he turned the key in the lock and flung the door wide, the light spilling out onto the cobbles.

"So you believed him but not me?" I asked as I stepped through, closely followed by the others.

"I'd recognise that bark anywhere. Hey, Anxious, did you have fun?"

Anxious rubbed against Bob's legs, then ran over to the bedding and sprawled out beside Babs who seemed unconcerned by the noise and was merrily drinking her wine. She tickled his tummy and he settled immediately, curling up in her lap and groaning before closing his eyes.

"Man, we need a better system," complained Carl, shooting an oblivious Bob the daggers before brushing past him and flopping onto the blankets.

"I thought it worked perfectly."

Bob beamed at us, then his smile faded as Babs called out, "How did it go? Did you find anything out?"

We explained what'd happened and the mood grew sombre; nobody knew quite what to make of it and now we were back together and hopefully safe for the night, the true extent of the weirdness began to envelope us in its chilly, rather terrifying embrace. It was so odd and downright freaky that we couldn't get to grips with it. How did everything tie together?

"So, what are we thinking?" asked Bob, eyelids drooping, cheeks as flushed as Babs', once more in the fuzzy Pinot embrace they both seemed to adore.

"That this is all about water. They've got a well and that's obviously where the water comes from. Somehow, and don't ask me how, there's something in it that sends you funny in the head. I'm guessing they've built up quite an immunity, although the new Pink didn't seem to have much trouble keeping up, but maybe he's been taking some away with him every time he visits so can handle as much as them."

"You think they murdered two men over the water?" asked Babs.

"Looks like it. Maybe Pink and the mystery man wanted to sell it or something. It's certainly got a punch. Or maybe the dead men were going to talk about it and the others refused and wanted it kept secret. Clearly nobody but them knows anything about it."

"But why the weird ritual in the cave?" asked Izzy, tucking a blanket up to her chin now we'd crawled onto the makeshift bed.

"Maybe the water only flows at night. Maybe it only happens on occasion. Or maybe it's tradition and part of living here. I honestly have no idea."

"We need to ask one of them in the morning," said Carl. "They can't all be the killer, so we should tell one of them that we know what they're up to with the water and see what the deal is."

"What if we pick the wrong person and they're the killer?" asked Izzy, making copious notes.

"It's a risk, sure, but what's the alternative? Wait around for someone to off us? No chance. We need information, and we need an ally. Maybe we should try one of the residents Max hasn't spoken to yet. We still have Red and Blue. Sure, they both looked like nutters, especially Red, so let's go knock on Blue's door early in the morning and see what he has to say."

"It is a risk," I said, nodding to Izzy in agreement, "but maybe Carl's right. We need to do something, and we need information if we're going to figure this out. So far we haven't learned much beyond they're weird and have a private well of what's basically magic water."

"Magic water! I like it," beamed Carl.

"But who warned you off the water?" asked Izzy. "You said it yourself that you drank it then blacked out and would have drowned if someone hadn't dragged you away from the shore. That means we already have an ally, doesn't it?"

"It does, but I have absolutely no idea who. Maybe there's someone else here we haven't encountered yet. After all, we still don't know who the mystery man is. He didn't have a boat, but White was adamant there were only five residents, so who is he?"

We looked towards the back where two bodies were currently residing in the storage room. By tomorrow, the smell would most likely be too much, and if we didn't get away we'd have to find somewhere else to spend the night. I shuddered at the thought.

No way did I want to spend another minute here, let alone another night.

Chapter 13

Everyone settled down as best they could, but I could tell by their breathing that they weren't asleep. Even Babs and Bob were restless; the alcohol wasn't enough to knock them out for more than a few minutes at a stretch.

The only one seemingly unconcerned was Anxious. He whimpered and snored merrily like he always did, legs twitching and repeatedly kicking everyone as he slowly shifted along our mess of blankets without waking once.

After untold minutes of this, I reluctantly sat up. The moment I did, the others joined me, waiting expectantly with raised eyebrows and hope in their eyes.

"What's the plan, Max?" asked Bob, grinning.

"Yes, what do we do?" asked Izzy. "I can't sleep, and clearly neither can anyone else. You thought of something, didn't you?"

"Actually, I didn't. I'm just restless and the, er, smell is getting a bit much. I need some fresh air."

"Oh, wow, I'm glad it's not just me," gushed Carl, flipping the blankets off his legs and jumping to his feet. "I was prepared to stay, but it does stink in here."

"Can't smell a thing," said Babs, eyes rather glassy.

"Me either," agreed Bob. "But I guess we're used to it." Bob sniffed, then nodded sagely. "Aye, that'll be decomposition setting in. Plus, you have all the bodily fluids that—"

"Mate, nobody wants to hear about that," grumbled Carl as he wagged a finger at Bob.

"It's just natural," shrugged Bob.

"I do really need some fresh air." I stood and joined Carl by the door, the air clearer, then thought for a moment before asking, "Does anyone want to come outside and risk it, or would you rather stay here? I'm going, but you can lock me out so you're safe, but I can't stay here all night."

Everyone wanted to come, even though I knew it wasn't the best idea. Still, I'd rather be outside with more places to run than locked in somewhere the killer might have a key for.

This was clearly not a night anyone would ever forget, and certainly not one for a good night's sleep, so once again we gathered a few things, this time including blankets and the rest of the booze, then Anxious and I checked the coast was clear before we regrouped outside the cafe and breathed deeply of the fresh, salty air.

My head cleared instantly, and I knew this was the right decision. Something had felt wrong inside the cafe, and I wasn't sure what. Maybe the bodies, possibly the smell, or the fact we were trapped. Whatever it was, being out in the open calmed my nerves and allowed me to think more clearly. Most likely, it was that Anxious and I had more room to ourselves.

I shook my head and chuckled at the thought, as we lived in a tiny vehicle with next to zero free space, and here I was feeling better because we weren't cramped. The difference was that in Vee I felt relaxed and at home, but in the cafe I felt nothing but apprehension. These people were strangers, after all, and how were you meant to relax and think clearly with people you didn't know farting and burping next to you? I glanced at Babs and Bob, the noxious culprits, and smiled when they noticed I was looking.

We wandered back to where they were sitting outside the cafe, and I asked if we could join them.

"Of course. Pull up a chair," said Bob, standing and scraping it back so I could sit.

"Thanks, Bob. That's very kind of you." I sat gratefully, and Anxious was in my lap and curled up in a flash.

"It's the least I could do after the way you've been looking after us. I mean it, Max, we do appreciate it. You're a great guy and have done so well leading this motley crew. Everyone says so."

"I haven't actually done anything," I sighed, rubbing at my cheeks to try to bring myself alive. "Luckily, nothing else bad has happened, although I was concerned in the cave."

"That sounds really weird," said Babs. "Were they really taking turns to drink and acting so strangely?"

"They were, and it was unsettling. I'm glad nobody spotted us. We just need to get through the night, then I'm sure help will arrive. That John guy from the boatyard must be wondering where his boats are and should have called the coastguard. If not, then my ex-wife or my parents will have. Hang in there, and don't worry. Help will arrive soon."

"Unless..." Bob trailed off, a deep frown creasing his tanned forehead.

"Yes?"

"Unless nobody has called anyone and we'll be stuck here until we get picked off one by one!" Bob grabbed Babs' hand and she huddled into him, clearly close to tears.

"That won't have happened. People will be worried, so help will come. Even if they weren't waiting to meet me, John the boat guy will be stressing about his business. Don't worry, everything will be fine."

"Tell that to the corpses." Bob shuddered and Babs whimpered. "Those markings have me worried, Max. That's not normal. Who does that? I mean, we've seen our fair share of terrible things over the years, but nothing so deranged. It's ritualistic and screams cult, and now here we are surrounded by a bunch of water-worshipping weirdos and we don't know who to trust or who's responsible."

"But we're going to find out."

"We are?" he asked, shocked.

"Oh yes. No way am I leaving this unresolved. I'm going to get to the bottom of this."

"I hope you do, but don't do anything that puts you in danger."

"I won't. At least not on purpose. Try to get some sleep. We'll stay here and wait until sunrise. Don't worry, Anxious will protect us."

"He's just tiny," said Babs.

"He may be small, but he's ferocious when it comes to looking after those he cares about. He'll bite anyone who tries anything."

"Thanks, Max." Babs eyelids fluttered and she leaned on Bob's shoulder then rested.

I nodded to Bob, who smiled weakly, then I went to sit on the harbour wall and think about things in peace.

Nothing came to mind, and I knew my racing thoughts would continue swirling around my head, so I changed tack and tried to think of nothing at all. It's not as easy as it seems. Meditation was something I had been trying to do every day to slow the thoughts until they stopped entirely, so I settled, began my breathing exercises, and gradually everything drifted away until I was left with no thoughts and only the faintest realisation there were others around me.

It was exactly what I needed, and the tension eased in my back and shoulders as I released all stress and concerns and settled into the present. After a while, thoughts surfaced once more, and somewhere in there I felt the beginnings of the truth start to stir and knew I would figure this out.

I was now so familiar with this sense of knowing but not knowing that I didn't try to push it, as that always meant I chased the insights away. So I simply accepted that I'd picked up on something somehow and in time I would solve this awful case and uncover the killer.

It gave me solace, and a grim sense of satisfaction, so I let it be and shook out my arms, rolled my head to loosen the taut muscles in my neck, then stood, leaving Anxious asleep on the blanket beside me.

As I turned to look at the cottages, I noticed that Izzy and Carl were sitting close together and talking quietly. It was good to see they were so friendly, as Carl had certainly not been very open when we'd first met. It seemed he was just a cautious guy who liked his own space, so didn't open up until he was sure he liked people. Admirable in many ways, as at least he didn't suffer fools gladly and pretend to enjoy the company of people he had no interest in. Maybe I should be more like that.

Was I a people pleaser? I didn't think so, but I was also rather polite when others were rude, and I wasn't sure if that was good or bad. Did they deserve to be treated with respect when they were the opposite? No, and I vowed that from now on I'd take a leaf out of Carl's book and refuse to pander to the vagaries of obtuse temperaments if it didn't suit me.

I turned away from them to the cottages and gasped.

Red and Blue were standing outside their front doors, staring at us impassively. Red still wore her incredible ballgown, whilst Blue wore nothing but a pair of cyan synthetic sports shorts. He had his arms crossed over his defined chest, and scowled as he watched us. Red was utterly devoid of expression, but her eyelids kept fluttering and she swayed as if listening to music only she could hear. Neither let their attention drift.

"Izzy, Carl," I whispered, then nodded to the islanders when I caught their attention.

Babs and Bob must have realised something was up, so came over to join us as we stood and turned to face the two dour residents.

"What are they doing?" asked Bob, shifting from foot to foot.

"I have no idea. Probably trying to intimidate us," I said, deciding I'd had enough of this nonsense and stepping forward with Anxious suddenly at my side, which buoyed my confidence.

"Hi. I was hoping to talk to you yesterday but—"

Red lifted a regal finger and placed it at her ruby lips, bringing attention to her wonky nose. Her eyes were two intense pinpoints of light, her face in shadow, making her cheeks appear even more hollow and her nose longer than it was. She adjusted her beret with her free hand, then shook wildly like a wet dog for no apparent reason. She laughed, lips curling in amusement, showing her large, crooked teeth, but there was an unmistakable air of elegance and upper-class roots to her that were unmistakable.

"Don't you silence them!" warned Blue in a deep baritone belying his years. His white hair shone pale yellow from the lights, as though he was going off like cheese left on the counter for days, his tan waxy under the sparse glow.

"And don't you dare talk to me that way!" hissed Red in a voice so posh and like something from a 50s BBC broadcast that it made everyone gasp. Nobody spoke that way nowadays, at least not in the company any of us kept.

With a dismissive wave of her hand towards Blue, Red stepped away from the threshold of her front door that seemed even smaller because of her six three size, and approached with a ruffle of her ballgown. She seemed to glide like she was on ice, her feet hidden as the gown swept the cobbles, then she paused halfway between us and the cottages and studied each of us in turn, taking her time.

"Check yourself, love." Bob's tone made me turn to him; he was visibly shaking. "Don't try to intimidate us, and don't look down on us either. You're screaming that you think you're better than us from every pore of your body and I can't stand that kind of attitude. Don't you dare act superior. I've met enough people like you in my time, and it won't work. So either be nice, or toddle back into your tiny house and leave us be."

Babs put her arm around Bob and pulled him close, then whispered something in his ear. He nodded, then left us and returned to the cafe and sat down, back to everyone.

"Excuse my husband, but he doesn't take kindly to people with obvious bad attitudes. In another life, he was a driver for a very well-to-do family and those upper-class twits and their friends treated him like a second-class citizen. He won't stand for any nonsense, and you won't get on with people with such a chip on your shoulder."

This was a side to Bob I'd never seen, and it shocked me as much as Izzy and Carl who were open-mouthed and silent until Carl laughed and shouted out, "Good for you, Bob."

"That shut you up," giggled Blue as he moved away from his house and stood on the cobbles, eyes dancing with mirth.

"Indeed. Most unexpected," said Red, regaining her composure and gliding closer. "That little man certainly has an issue with his betters, but I'm sure he'll come around once he knows how wonderful I am."

"Betters?" I asked, incredulous. "Are you seriously saying that you're better than him? At what? Life? Love? Friendships? What makes you superior?"

"Breeding, dear boy. Breeding." Red focused on me, and it was clear she was trying to intimidate me just like everyone else. A self-confidence born of schooling, strict upbringing, and certainly living a life of luxury far removed from all but a tiny minority. Yet here she was, hidden away in a tiny cottage, not talking to her neighbours, dressed in red, and sneaking off in the middle of the night to perform weird rituals around wells. It made no sense. This whole place made no sense.

"Ignore her. She's a posh fool who thinks she's better than everyone else." Blue teased Red with a cheesy grin then approached, before stopping when Anxious growled and barred his way. "Guess I haven't made the best impression either. Who are you people? What are you doing here?"

"You don't know?" I asked, not really surprised.

"I heard there was an issue with Pink, and now we have a new one. A brother, but he isn't the most talkative of guys and we only had a quick word."

"What is wrong with you people?" demanded Carl. "Old Pink is dead. Murdered. We found this other guy trussed up like a scarecrow, and he's dead too. Someone nobbled the boats so we can't leave, and there's a killer on the loose."

"Nonsense!" hissed Red, joining us.

Anxious turned his attention to her and upped his growling level to ten. He did not like this woman at all.

"Control your mutt or I shall kick it into the water."

"If you try, he'll bite your ankle, and I'll personally shove you over the side," I told her calmly.

"Indeed! How dare you!" With a dramatic flourish, she spun and glided back to her house, opened the door, then went inside and slammed it shut.

"Ignore her. She's always like that. In case you didn't know, we don't exactly get on like good neighbours around here."

"So we heard," I said, surprised Blue was being so talkative.

"Yeah. I bet!" he laughed, seemingly genuinely friendly.

"Do you mind talking to us for a while? We have a lot of questions."

"Sure. But what I want to know is why you're here at this ungodly hour. This isn't the place to hang around, especially now. Why are you on my island?" There was a definite undertone of annoyance, but I ignored that as he seemed relatively normal, if rather unfocused. That would be the water, I reminded myself. He, and the others, were most likely far from clearheaded.

"Like we just said, there's been two murders, the boats have been sunk, and the speedboat's had its wiring ruined."

"I heard about it from new Pink. He's a dumb brute and I'm not sure it will work out here for him, but he's been coming here for years on and off to see his brother and try to convince him to leave, but mostly he comes for the… Anyway, forget about that. If someone's killed old Pink and some random, you'd best find a way to get off this rock."

"You aren't concerned?"

"Let me tell you all one very important thing." Blue stepped closer and we gathered round, even Bob who'd decided to join us now Red had left. "People die here on a regular basis. Sometimes it's natural, other times not. It's the way of the island. If you live here, you come to expect it. Don't get me wrong, it's not an everyday occurrence, or even every year, but every decade or two, someone pops their clogs and then a replacement turns up. It is what it is." Blue shrugged, unconcerned.

"Why would you possibly live somewhere when there's so much risk involved?" asked Izzy.

"Because it has its own special kind of beauty. There's nowhere else like this in the whole world. It's special, and it takes a special kind of person to live here and handle the isolation and the damn annoying neighbours. We have traditions that go back centuries, possibly even further. It is what it is." Again, he shrugged.

"It's the water, isn't it?" I asked, unable to let this go now we finally had someone who would answer at least a few questions.

Blue lunged for me, grabbed me by the throat with incredibly strong hands, and got right up in my face and demanded, "What do you know about the water?"

Chapter 14

"Hands off!" I hissed, then bunched my fists and slammed down with all my might onto his forearms.

Blue's grip went slack as he screamed and backed away, clutching first one forearm then another. His eyes welled from the pain and his dark skin turned puce as he shook out his arms and I rubbed at my neck, my eyes never straying from him for a moment.

"You broke my arms!" he squealed, his bravado dissipating like Anxious' noxious farts on a windy day.

"They aren't broken. Nothing snapped. What do you think you were doing? You could have strangled me. What is wrong with you people?"

"You do not talk about the water," mumbled Blue. "Ever. It's the rules. Nobody ever discusses the water. What do you know of it?" He inspected his arms, then sighed when he flexed his fingers and realised the bones weren't broken.

"Are you okay?" asked Carl, Bob beside him, both with their fists up, ready to fight, which I found admirable.

Izzy and Babs were on Blue's left, and looking even more capable. Izzy was in a fighting stance and she looked like she knew how to fight, and Babs had a bottle of wine raised, ready to clobber Blue if he tried anything again.

"I'm fine. Thanks for having my back." I nodded to my new friends then turned my attention to Blue.

"We need to have a serious talk. Let's calm down, but you've got some explaining to do. If you don't want the police going through every square inch of your home looking for murder weapons or clues, then you need to explain exactly what's going on here and help us figure out who did it. And I am not saying that you're in the clear. For all we know, it was you."

"It wasn't me! Why would I murder Pink then get stuck with his idiot brother? And I don't even know who the other man is."

"Then let's start there. Can we go back inside please so we can show Blue the body? He might recognise him."

"I don't care who he is. I just want to be left alone. You need to go."

Carl stepped forward and said, "We already told you. We can't leave. The boats have sunk."

"Fine." Blue looked defeated as he led the way to the cafe then waited while it was opened. We crowded in and Bob locked it behind us with a rather ominous clunk.

None of the others were keen to go into the back, but as I led the way, Izzy suddenly brushed past Blue and said, "I'm coming too," a determined look in her eyes.

"Are you sure? You don't need to."

"I've been so stressed since this happened, and I'm getting seriously freaked out by all this weird stuff. I want to make things feel more normal, you know?"

"Kind of," I admitted.

"If I can look at the men, it might make it feel more real and less like a dream. Plus, I didn't actually get a proper look at the stranger earlier. I've been in the area for over a week now and been seeing the sights, but also hanging out very close as that's where I'm camping. Maybe I'll recognise him and that will give us something to go on."

"That's a smart idea. Blue, are you ready?"

"Why wouldn't I be?" he asked, stifling a yawn.

"Because it's a corpse?" I suggested.

"I've seen my fair share over the years. Much worse than anything you could show me. I used to be in the army, spent two decades seeing the worst of humanity. The odd stiff here every few years is nothing."

We entered the storage room and stopped at the bodies. Blue and I uncovered Pink first, but there was little point apart from to confirm it was him. Next was the mystery man, and when I pulled back the tarp Izzy gasped, but Blue was stoic and just bent to study his face then inspect the strange motif carved into the poor man's flesh.

"What's that all about?"

"We were hoping you could tell us. Does it mean anything to you?"

"A circle with what looks like a knife or an arrow through it and those weird squiggles? It means nothing. It's like a doodle. No, wait! Yes, that's it! I think I know what this is." Blue stood and laughed, clearly unaffected by the bloated corpse or the wounds inflicted on this man of mystery.

"I don't recognise him," said Izzy, turning away with a hand to her face as her cheeks flushed.

"That's okay." I put my arm to her shoulder from behind and asked, "Do you want to return to the front?"

"No. I want to hear what Blue has to say. First, I'd like to know your real name."

Blue's smile faded. "We don't use our old names here. They're a thing of the past. All that remains of the man I once was is this body. I am Blue. Nothing more." He was determined, that was clear, and when we nodded that we understood he continued. "I do know what that symbol is though."

"What?" we asked eagerly.

"It's one of those things Green uses. What does she call them? Dreamcatchers. Load of nonsense if you ask me, but she's always wandering around with one of them or some other daft item she reckons she can use to harness energy. She's a right madwoman that one. Has loads of rocks, and her staff she swears stores up energy because she fixed a crystal on the end of it, too, and all kinds of nonsense."

"But you've seen this exact symbol? How did she make it from a dreamcatcher?"

"It's just feathers and sticks and little stones and stuff," he said with a shrug. "The one she's always wafting about looks like this. Black crow's feathers around a circle of twigs, then driftwood to make a kind of sword thing with two arms coming off it and lots of bits dangling beneath it. It's the same."

"I think you're describing a general dreamcatcher," I said, thinking of the ones I'd seen in the various boho shops I'd frequented on my travels, many of the items identical from shop to shop.

"No, this one's different, and she's always shoving it in our faces and telling us she'll gain our power. Anyway, up to you. I'm not about to go knocking on her door. She's an utter loon."

"Thanks for your help. Now, about the water?"

"What about it?" he asked gruffly, his emotions shutting down and his body language changing to that of a man who was not going to share more than the bare minimum until he could get away.

"Let's go back to the others so everyone can hear. And we want proper answers. People are dead and something strange is going on here. We want to know what. Our lives may depend on it."

"Don't be so dramatic," he laughed, slapping me on the back, suddenly acting like we were best friends." Blue wandered off, leaving Izzy and I to cover up the body, confused by his ever-changing mood.

"I think he's a little off-kilter. Possibly PTSD from his time in the army," said Izzy.

"Or his time here. They all seem the same. Not quite with it. As some would say, they seem away with the fairies."

"They really do, don't they?" she giggled, her spirits lifting now Blue had left.

"Are you sure you're alright? It's a lot to see a corpse close up like that. Especially one that's been so brutalised."

"I think I'm okay. Yes, I am. I'm glad I came to see. Um, not glad. Sorry, but you know what I mean."

"I do. And thanks for helping to get Blue to talk. Let's go and see what he has to say now."

Blue was standing in the middle of the cafe, looking bemused. Probably because Babs and Bob were snuggled under the blankets with Anxious sitting between them. He wagged when he saw me, but stayed put, eyes on Blue, guarding everyone at once as best he could whilst remaining snuggly.

The two undertakers were merrily slurping wine, which I found astonishing considering the fact it was now early morning and they'd been at it since who knew when the day before. Most likely since the morning, as they seemed to take their boozing very seriously. But hey, they were on holiday, and this was a high-stress situation. I could have done with a few more glasses myself.

Carl, on the other hand, was still sitting at one of the tables we'd pushed aside to make room for our bed. He was leaning forward in his chair, elbows on the table, palms cupping his head, eyes locked on Blue. He looked exhausted, and I assumed he was in that position so he could remain awake.

"Blue is going to explain about the water," I told everyone. They became instantly alert, so I told Blue, "I drank a bottle of water from here, then collapsed on the beach. I would have drowned if someone hadn't dragged me to safety. They left a note saying not to drink the water. I couldn't figure it out until everyone felt peculiar after dinner yesterday, and that was just because I used a splash to make stock."

"What did you have?"

"Pardon?"

"For dinner? Was it nice? I'm not much of a cook myself, and never seem to have the time."

"No time?" asked Carl. "What do you do all day?"

Blue shrugged. "Not sure. Fish, sunbathe, walk. Think. The usual."

"And get off your trolley on the water," giggled Babs.

"Yeah, that's some good stuff. We were high as kites after Max's dinner. And it was boiled."

"It is potent, yes," agreed Blue, seemingly resigned to giving us the information we craved.

"We saw you," I admitted, deciding it was best to come clean. Blue was certainly a suspect—there weren't many residents after all—but maybe this would tease more information from him and he'd let something slip or prove his innocence. Either way, I figured that we had nothing to lose and if he tried anything in here we could easily overpower him.

"Doing what? And do you mind if I sit?"

"Help yourself," said Carl, dragging out a chair.

Blue sat with a grateful sigh, and explained, "My knees aren't what they used to be. The right one hurts something awful after I stand for a while, and it's been a long night so far."

"Enough about the knees," screeched Izzy, startling everyone. "Sorry, but this is nuts. Will you just explain about the water so we can try to rest? Everyone's exhausted, and I just want to close my eyes and not feel terrified that someone's going to murder one of us."

"There are no killers amongst the residents," insisted Blue. "Crazies, sure. But killers, no. Believe what you want. But I know them."

"You don't know the new Pink," I noted.

"I know him well enough. I told you, he's been coming here for years."

"For the water."

"Yes, for the water. It's special. You say you saw us. Where exactly?"

"In the cave."

"Then you know our secret. That's not good, and you shouldn't tell the others. We've gone to a lot of trouble over the years to ensure that our secret remains just that. They won't take kindly to strangers spying on them. Neither do I."

"What you going to do about it?" demanded Bob from his prone position, bottle of wine poised to drink.

"Um, nothing, I guess. I can't say the same for the others, which is why I said not to tell them. Look, I don't know who the mystery guy is, and I don't care. What I do care about is you not spoiling it for us here. Yes, it's the water that keeps us here."

"What's in it?" I asked.

"No idea. Nobody does. It's magical."

Bob sniggered, but Blue ignored him.

"You don't believe that," said Izzy.

"Not in the way Green does. She thinks it really is a spiritual thing. Real magic. Me, I'm a pragmatist. I even got it tested once, top secret stuff, and nothing was found that could explain the effects. And trust me, they are profound. Sure, there's a cerebral side to it which is far from unpleasant, but it's the other things it does that make it so special."

"Where does it come from?" I wondered.

"The well has always been here and nobody knows who built it or even if it's just a natural occurrence. A fault line in the rock, a natural spring. The pump gets renewed every so often, but it's tradition that it's done manually. Once a week we gather around and take our personal fill straight from the tap, then fill up containers and whatnot. It's how it's always been done."

"What does it actually do to you?"

"Knocks you out if you aren't used to it. We all are. It gives you a strange high that's hard to explain. Like being drunk but without the hangover or the loss of your sensibilities. But after a while that isn't very intense. It's more an all-body thing. It just makes you feel invincible and like you could do anything. Live forever type of feeling that lasts almost an entire week. It cures you of all the aches and pains, the little niggles you didn't even know you had, and leaves you feeling awesome." Blue beamed at us, like he'd just spread the best news ever, but when we didn't react he looked confused. "You don't believe me?"

"Blue, you told us your knee is giving you issues. That doesn't sound like the water is so great."

"I may have been lying about that. I'm fine, actually. I only said that to put you at ease and so you wouldn't feel as threatened. Plus, I like sitting down," he chuckled, amused by his own joke.

"This is getting us nowhere," said Carl. "Are you seriously telling us that you all live here even though you can't stand the sight of each other, because of the water?"

"It's the most incredible thing I've ever encountered. Believe me or not, I honestly don't care, but it makes you feel truly alive in ways I never even dreamed of. It's worth the hardships and then some."

"Worth killing to protect?" I asked, an idea forming.

"I never said that!"

"Maybe the mystery man was invited here by one of the residents and he was going to see about bottling and selling it. It's an idea that's been forming for a while and now it feels like it might be the answer. Did you invite that man here to see how much you could get, Blue, but someone found out and murdered him?"

"Don't be ridiculous. I'd never let our secret out and neither would anyone else. Our whole way of life would be ruined. The place would be overrun and we'd never be able to live here. Everything would fall apart and where would I go then? Without access to the water, I'd be dead in weeks."

"That's rather an extreme exaggeration," I said.

"Not when you're ninety-seven years old, it isn't," he snapped, then slapped a hand over his mouth.

The room fell deathly silent as we stared at him, astounded, and incredulous.

Chapter 15

"Ignore that," he said hurriedly, ruffling his grey, but now I took more notice, surprisingly thick head of hear. For a moment I wondered if he actually dyed it to look older. Would he? "Just a little joke." A forced laugh escaped his pursed lips, and his Adam's apple bobbed as he swallowed.

"You were fooling around, right?" asked Izzy nervously. "I mean, I know people can live a long time, but you don't look a day over sixty-five or so."

"Of course I was teasing. As if! Time for me to go. But heed my warning and leave this place. The others don't take kindly to strangers, and you've all outstayed your welcome. Don't snoop on us, don't try to pin the deaths on any of us, and do not," Blue grew serious as he wagged a finger, "ever, and I mean ever, tell a soul about the water."

"Or what?" asked Carl. "I don't like people threatening me. I've had it with this place, and all the crap you people get up to. Magic water and lies about your age? It's incredible. I think living here and being so isolated has sent you funny in the head. You need to get back to civilisation."

"Believe what you want. It makes zero difference to me. As for civilisation, that's exactly why we live here. To escape it all. If John would stop renting out his stupid boats, we'd be happy. But he won't listen and reckons it's good for us to have visitors. Keeps us in touch with the outside world, he says, but really he just wants to line his pockets."

"Maybe he's right. Maybe you do need contact with others. I understand the appeal. I live in my van full-time so know what it's like to be isolated, but you need people. Maybe it would be different if you got on with your neighbours. A proper community rather than whatever this is you have going on. It isn't healthy."

"Ah, a vanlifer." Blue smiled warmly at me and relaxed, now seemingly keen to continue a conversation he'd wanted to cut short only a moment ago. "I remember that life well. Loved it. I spent years living in a converted military vehicle as I couldn't settle in a house after the army. I was too restless and had the roaming bug, so travelled all over."

"But you gave that life up to move here?"

"You've got to understand this was a very long time ago. I began in the fifties, then into the sixties. It got more common then. Mostly dropouts and hippies looking for a different way of life. I met some amazing people and had some great times. Man, it was such a cool vibe back then for several years, but it turned sour in the end like most things do. Then I heard talk of this place. It was always discussed in hushed tones, and this was before there were rental boats to get here, but I found a way and couldn't believe it when I discovered an empty cottage and moved straight in. I'm the oldest resident by a few years. Not many, but a few, then along came some of the others when the old residents died. And before you ask, no, they didn't get murdered. At least, I don't think so." Blue was lost to his own thoughts for a while, and we did nothing but look at each other in confusion and wonder, unsure if he was just a fanciful man or there was truth in his words.

"I think I'll stick to vanlife," I laughed, my mind whirling with Blue's revelations.

"We're the same, you and I," insisted Blue. "Max, you gave up conventional life because it didn't satisfy you, right?"

"True."

"Let me guess. You had a beautiful home life, but it wasn't enough. You were always chasing something better, something more. That elusive something you didn't even understand. Caught up in the grind, the daily obsession with work, never realising what you had right in front of you the whole time. I bet it blew up in your face at some point and you slowly came to realise that it was all a con. That what you'd been led to believe was how things should be done, how you should live, was a lie. A deceit."

"I wouldn't put it quite like that, and to be honest even though I adore vanlife I'd give it up if it meant getting the love of my life back. I know what's important, and it's not where you live, or what you live in, but who you live with. And that's the one thing you're overlooking here, Blue, with your insistence on this being the perfect life you lead. You failed to accept that it's the people that make it beautiful, not the location, and certainly not the water."

"You don't understand," he mumbled. Without another word, and shaking his head, he marched to the door, turned the key, then left.

I locked up behind him, then faced the others.

"Do you believe him?" asked Izzy, then everyone began chattering loudly and talking over each other, their excitement and utter bewilderment equal to mine.

"He's nuts," said Carl. "You can't live that long and look like him. He was lying, right?"

"Maybe he was telling the truth," I admitted. "But one thing I do know is that he was wrong about the rest. This is no way to live. None of them are happy. We've seen that with our own eyes. They hate each other, despise people coming here, and can't stand almost everything about their way of life. They're addicts, plain and simple, and the only reason they stay is because the water has something in it that messes with your head."

"I agree with Max. All of them are utterly crazy. Only a true addict would live the way they do and put up with this madness. What's the point? I'd get it if they were happy here and just wanted to be left alone to enjoy it. That's not what this is."

"What is it then?" asked Carl.

"A hellhole," said Izzy softly. "An utter hellhole. None of these people are nice, not a single one of them enjoys their life, and look what it's done to them. They're out of their minds. The water's eaten away at them until what's left is something gross. It's vile and we have to get away from here."

"I agree. I'm going back outside. There's no way I'm going to sleep tonight and it'll be dawn soon enough."

Once again, the others agreed with me, so with wine and soft drinks in hand, as there was no way I'd risk making a coffee even with the water being boiled, we exited.

The only one unhappy with the decision was Anxious, who groaned and tried the old puppy dog sad eyes trick on me so he could be left alone with the massive makeshift bed. He was a good boy, though, and once I asked him politely, and possibly the promise of a biscuit had something to do with his change of heart, he trotted outside and sat waiting patiently for me to lock up.

"What now?" asked Bob.

I gave Anxious his biscuits then focused on Bob. "Now we really do need to find a way off this place. I'm going back to the jetty to look over what we've got left and see if I can come up with something."

"Max, there's nothing there but the speedboat. The wiring's shot and none of us can fix that without getting to the mainland and finding a professional. The other boats have sunk."

"Yes, I know, and in truth I just need time alone to think. Do you mind?"

"Hell no!" he laughed. "We've been living on top of each other and I think all of us need some space. I'll have a word with the others, explain things, and don't worry, I'll insist nobody wanders off, but we can spread out as long as we stay in range. Agreed?"

"Yes, absolutely," I said hurriedly, immensely relieved. "Thanks, Bob. You're a great friend, even if a very new one."

"I feel the same way, Max. I like you, and who knows what would have happened without you here with us."

"You'd have been fine. I haven't done anything."

"That's where you're wrong. You've done a lot for us. Kept everyone together, and safe, and I can tell that you're itching to figure this out. Think you will?"

"I do. There's something we've overlooked that will reveal itself in time. But right now the only thing I know for certain is that I'm never coming back here."

"Now that's something we can all agree on," he chuckled, then saluted and left to explain to the others what would happen next.

The sense of relief was immeasurable as Anxious and I wandered over to the end of the jetty then sat. With my legs dangling over the edge, after I removed my Crocs just in case I lost one in the water, and with Anxious curled up beside me, I let the peace envelop me. Dawn would be here soon enough, and with it a newfound hope, as the darkness plays funny tricks on your mind and everything gets blown out of proportion. Not that we weren't in a truly dire predicament, I admitted that, but somehow I knew we were safe, although I couldn't exactly figure out why.

Were the residents tucked up in bed, or were they watching and waiting, ready to strike? Maybe they were in on it together and had eliminated Pink for whatever reason. The same for the other man. Or it was just one of them and the truth would never be uncovered. The other possibility was that it was someone who had committed the crimes then simply left by boat and they'd got away with it and would never be found.

All of this was possible, and yet somehow I knew the answer lay elsewhere. With time to think without interruption, and the stress receding now I wasn't so on edge, which was possibly because of the deep tiredness I felt, I let it all go and stared out to sea.

Again, I heard strange voices on the wind, and scanned the area for signs of life, but there was nothing but gulls. What a way to live. Was Blue right and we were alike? Both escaping the regular world to live unconventional lives away from others? No. He was wrong. I'd interacted with more people in the last few months than I had in the preceding few years, and loved that aspect of vanlife.

My thoughts were interrupted once more by the sound of voices out to sea, and I could have sworn it was my parents. The water must still be messing with my head, I assumed, but suddenly Anxious sat upright, eyes glued to the water, and his tail began to wag as he sniffed the air.

I followed his gaze and to my astonishment I saw a small rowing boat come around the headland and approach slowly. The sun rose as I stood, so I shielded my eyes and saw one of the most bizarre sights I had ever witnessed.

Oars splashed without rhythm into the still water, the back of a man bent over and constantly mistiming his stroke, but that wasn't what had me burst into a fit of laughter I feared I might never be able to stop. What left me in uncontrollable fits of merriment was the sight of my mother, resplendent in a black, fifties dress with more ruffles than at Crufts, covered in huge red polka dots. She was standing proud at the stern, bare arms on her hips, her red hair mostly covered by a bandanna that matched her dress. Mum's hand lifted to shade her eyes as she shouted, "Cooee. Max, it's me. Your mum."

"He knows who you are, you big idiot," Dad snapped, loosing what momentum he had and flapping about in the boat as he tried to get the oars back into the water.

"Don't you call me big. Or an idiot," Mum added as an afterthought. "Are you saying I'm fat?"

"Course not, love. You aren't fat."

"Oh, so I was fat? Is that what you're saying?"

"Don't be daft. I'm saying you look lovely, and of course Max wanted you to remind him that you're his mother."

"That's alright then," she said with a smile then a frown Dad chose to ignore, deciding to focus on his rowing.

"Max! Max, it's us. Mum and Dad."

"Hi!" I hollered, beyond relieved to see them, knowing that finally we could escape and be done with this terrible place.

"Stop rocking the boat!" roared Dad as he redoubled his efforts and managed, for a few brief strokes of the oars, to get the timing right and actually get closer to the jetty.

"I'm not. It's you and your rubbish driving."

"It's not driving. It's rowing. Sit down!"

With a wave and a blown kiss for me, Mum sat, almost tipping them over as she faffed about until Dad turned and grabbed her to steady them.

"Don't you grab me like that, you fool. I nearly went overboard. Do you know how much this dress cost? It would have been ruined."

"You said it was cheap in the sales and the assistant said you looked so pretty that she gave you extra discount so it was practically free."

Mum mumbled something that I couldn't hear and I guessed Dad couldn't either, and my grin broadened as they got closer and closer. I hurriedly snatched a rope and as Dad made another effort to steer the boat but couldn't synchronise his stroke, resulting in them turning to face the wrong way, he began rowing back out to sea.

"Turn around!" I yelled, panic setting in.

"I did."

"No, the other way. You have to have your back to us."

"Stupid way to row, if you ask me. How are you supposed to know which way you're going?"

"Just focus," I told him as our eyes met and his smile warmed my heart.

"Right you are." With a nod, Dad managed to turn the boat by using a single oar, then rowed a little closer.

"Mum, get ready to grab the rope."

"Which rope, love?" she asked, utterly composed and looking like she was having a jolly time.

"The one in my hand. I'm going to throw it to you."

"Why would I want a rope?"

"Not the whole thing. Just one end. I'll tie the other to the jetty and you wrap your end around that piece of metal there and that way you can't float away."

"Aw, you're so smart. Isn't he clever, Jack? Such a good boy."

"Mum, it's how you do it. This is what everyone does."

"Is it? Then you aren't so smart." She laughed, winking so I'd know she was teasing.

I threw the rope, but she failed to catch it, moving away rather than reaching out for it. I hauled it in to try again, but this time she batted it away like it was dangerous.

"You have to catch it."

"It's dirty and stinky. Don't worry, we'll be fine. Just grab the boat and hold us steady."

Knowing it was a lost cause with the rope, I lay on my front and somehow gripped the boat as they got close enough.

"Hello, love," beamed Mum as she stood, then stepped cautiously onto the ladder.

Anxious was going out of his mind, barking and whimpering, keen to say hello and possibly get a treat for being so awesome. The others had gathered around too.

Carl reached out to help Mum, and he hauled her up onto the jetty where she thanked him then brushed herself down, more concerned about her dress than anything else.

"Dad, you need to hurry. I can't hold on to the boat much longer. Izzy, can you tie the rope onto the boat please?"

"Sure thing." Izzy picked up one end then bent to secure the line, but Dad took that moment to abandon the oars and stand.

The boat rocked wildly and Izzy missed her chance, and Dad panicked then slumped down. My arms were screaming now, the strain getting too much, then the boat drifted and I had to let go.

"Dad, get closer so Izzy can tie the rope."

"Right you are." He settled on the bench seat then grabbed the oars and managed a few effective strokes.

I reached out once again, took hold of the stern, and Dad let go of the oars, which began to slide down from their holdings.

"Dad, grab the oars! Pull them into the boat or they'll slip through those rings. We need them."

To everyone's immense relief, he did as I asked. Dad stood, Izzy readied with the rope, and I held on for dear life.

"Here we go," he laughed, then stumbled to the rear and jumped.

"No!" everyone shouted.

Pushing back with his one foot on the boat while the other made contact with the jetty, Dad's force made my grip give out, and as the boat glided out to sea Dad took hold of the rope Izzy held so she yanked him backwards and they fell in a heap.

I watched in horror as the boat drifted away slowly, but readied to go in after it when the current caught and our only hope of salvation sped away in seconds, way too far out to sea for me to have a hope of going after it and surviving.

"Hello, Son," beamed Dad as he stood and helped Izzy to her feet.

"What a lovely day," said Mum with a grin.

"I've had better," I sighed.

Chapter 16

For one blissful moment I stared at the horizon as the orange ball of fire rose above the calm waters, turning everything gloriously pink. Clouds caught the rays and burst into life, and so did the wildlife. Gulls screeched, fish broke the surface, sending ripples out in ever-increasing circles, then silence enveloped me and I was mesmerised by the world's beauty. It was hard to imagine that the sun was 93 million miles away and 1.3 million earths could fit inside the fiery orb. Astonishing, and impossible to truly comprehend.

It put everything into perspective, and I was at peace as my eyes drifted to the tiny speck of a boat that moments ago had been our salvation.

"Son?" Dad put his hand to my shoulder and I exited my trance, unsure how long I'd been standing there, but noting that somehow the sun had risen completely above the horizon now and was hanging there like a magical ball, low in the sky but dawn had well and truly broken.

"Sorry, I forgot how spectacular the sunrise can be."

"That's alright. Sometimes we need a moment to ourselves. Are you okay, Max? You've been standing like that for ten minutes and nobody could get you to answer. We blew it, didn't we? Same old story. I'm sorry."

"Hey, there's nothing to be sorry about. We'll figure something out."

"What exactly has been going on here? Is everything okay or are you in trouble? We were worried, so figured we'd better come and check on you. It, er, took a while longer than we expected."

"Got lost, did you?" I teased, knowing how bad they were with directions.

"Just for a while," he laughed, relief washing over him now I was communicating again.

"Thanks for coming. Sorry about ignoring you. I think it was the shock of seeing the boat drift off. Now we're still stuck here."

"There's a great big boat right there," he said with a frown, indicating the speedboat.

"It's been messed with. All the wiring's been ripped out."

"Oh, and where are the rowing boats?"

"Stop hogging my son!" Mum shoved Dad aside and flung herself forward, gripping me in a tight hug. It felt awesome, and just what I needed. "It's alright now, Max. Mum's here," she whispered into my ear.

I didn't have the heart to tell her that all this did was complicate things, so instead held her tight and enjoyed the closeness. You can never beat a hug from your mum, whatever age you are. "It's great to see you. It's been the longest night of my life."

Mum pulled back, looked me in the eye, and asked, "What happened?"

"I think you better sit down before I tell you," I chuckled, sighing. "Have you said hello to Anxious?" I turned to see him with Dad getting a fuss, whilst the others milled about, looking uncertain about what to do. Babs was crying as she stared out to sea, most likely distraught about the boat.

"We've been here for over ten minutes, love," said Mum, clearly confused. "We've played with Anxious and everyone introduced themselves, but your friends said they'd wait until you were ready then explain what's been going on. Are you okay? That's not like you to ignore us when we've had so much trouble getting here."

"I'm sorry. I think I had an existential crisis when the boat drifted away. Sorry, Mum." I kissed the top of her head, the familiar Mum smell making me smile, then she took my hand and squeezed tightly.

"It's no bother. You do what you need to. I'm sure you've had an awful time of it and then we turn up and cause trouble and lose the boat. At least we managed to stay afloat all night." Mum giggled, looking cheery, but she had telltale bags under her eyes and it was obvious she was exhausted. I'd been lax to not notice, and now I studied her properly it was clear she was far from her usual immaculate condition.

Her makeup had faded and not been re-applied, the hair poking out from beneath the bandanna was slightly unruly, and her dress was rumpled. Her bright red high heels, however, were spotless and I could picture her hunkering down in the boat and rubbing them clean as she hated dirty shoes.

I turned to check on Dad and he was showing signs of a hard night too. His white T-shirt with the sleeves rolled up to show off his biceps was grubby, his slicked back, greased hair in the fifties style he and Mum were obsessed with was messy and looked dry, something I hadn't seen in years, and the turn-ups on his 501s had bunched up and were filthy from the boat.

"I think we need to have a chat and find out what's been going on with you guys," I said.

"Great idea! Can we get a cup of tea? I'm parched. We ran out of water and it's been a very long night."

"How long were you out there for?" I asked, aghast at the thought of them floating around forever and dying of thirst.

"A long, long time." Mum smiled weakly, then her face flushed and she fell into my arms, unconscious.

"Dad!"

Together, we lay Mum down as she regained consciousness and batted at Dad, insisting she was fine, but it was clear the ordeal had taken a lot out of them both. After a few minutes to recover, she was able to stand so we trailed back to the cafe where Babs and Bob cleared away the bedding then sorted out the tables and chairs so everyone could sit down and we could explain what had happened and my folks could tell their sorry tale.

And what a tale it was.

Everyone was keen to hear, so after I explained briefly without too much detail why there was no running water but we still had sealed bottles I could use to make a brew, and then made everyone a cuppa, we settled down to hear the incredulous tale of why two people who had always been incapable of reading maps or following the simplest of directions decided to get in a rowing boat and try to rescue me.

It had, as it obviously would, gone horribly wrong. For a start, Dad couldn't get the hang of rowing and kept going around in circles. Once he'd mastered the art, his words, not mine, and judging by Mum's eye rolls he absolutely had not got the hang of it at all, it began to get dark. Regardless, they carried on towards the island, or what they thought was the island, but it was pitch black by the time they arrived only to discover it wasn't the island at all, but an outcropping of rocks with no way to moor and nothing but seagulls there anyway.

They navigated as best they could, working out which way to go by the lights shining along the coast, hoping to get back to shore and start again in the morning. But the currents were strong, and Dad was tired, so Mum took over for a while and rather than head back she was determined to find me so rowed in the direction she figured was right and Dad agreed they should at least try to find me.

As night wore on, they realised it was a lost cause and decided to go back to shore, but the current was too strong and every time they rested they drifted back out to sea.

With no reception, their phones were useless, so they rowed and rowed, taking turns, and eventually they happened to see the lights from the island and with it came a renewed sense of hope.

After several failed attempts where they got close only to be beaten back because of exhaustion, they finally got a second wind as dawn approached, and managed to approach the jetty. The rest we knew.

"So we made it!" said Mum brightly, looking better and clearly feeling it now she'd had a few cuppas and even managed to freshen up and re-apply her make-up.

"You could have died out there," Babs admonished with a tut then a cuddle for Mum. They'd hit it off straight away and now seemed like best friends.

"It will take more than a stupid boat and some water to get the better of me," laughed Mum, seemingly enjoying herself immensely now.

"She's right, Mum, that was so dangerous. Once you became worried, why not call the coastguard? And is Min alright? Where is she?"

"Probably sleeping in Vee. We met her at the campsite and she was already worried because she hadn't heard from you, so we went down to where you got the boat from but they were closed up and we didn't know how to contact the owner. Then we found this other place where we managed to rent a boat, but we insisted Min stay behind in case you turned up."

"So she's safe?" I asked, beyond relieved.

"Sure. And so is Vee, your beloved campervan," teased Dad with a wink.

"But why not call the coastguard?"

"We assumed you'd lost track of time," said Mum. "It wasn't that late, so we hired a boat to come and meet you and take a look at the island. It seems nice. I love the cottages. Not much going on here, though, is there?"

"There's more going on than you'd believe," I sighed.

"Time for you to tell us the full tale," said Dad with a nod. "And what happened to your boats and why has the speedboat had the wiring ripped out?"

"Dad, I don't even know where to begin."

"Start with the murder," he laughed, eyes glinting. "There's always a murder, so I'm guessing that's why you're still here. We knew it, didn't we, Jill?"

"Of course we did. That's why we came once we realised you weren't back to meet us. We convinced Min that it was probably nothing, but she knew there was trouble, same as us. She'll be going spare by now, I bet."

"Thanks for that," I sighed, stress levels rising.

"You're welcome." Mum grinned, oblivious to sarcasm as always.

"So," encouraged Dad, "who got killed and who's the killer? What's been going on here? And what's this about the water?"

It took some time to explain everything as Mum and Dad weren't keen on sitting and listening quietly, preferring to interrupt constantly and give their advice on what should have been done and offering unsolicited opinions on who was most likely to have committed the crimes. They even asked if they could try the special water to see if it was as good as Blue said it was.

Everyone explained why that wasn't a good idea, but they took a lot of convincing and Dad especially seemed desperate to experience it firsthand until I told him what had happened to me and how I'd nearly drowned but was saved by a mystery person.

"So how do we get out of here?" asked Mum, looking nervous.

"We can't. It's why I went a little funny after you lost your boat. You were our only hope. I know I shouldn't say this, as I don't want to worry anyone, but we need to face facts and admit that the killer may well strike again. They're on the island with us and we don't know who they are."

"Son, they might have had a boat and just left," said Dad casually, relaxed and utterly unconcerned.

"I don't think so."

"Why?"

"Because this place is so small that we'd have seen a boat if someone left."

"They could have got away without you seeing," he insisted. "None of you have been keeping a constant lookout, and the killings might have been committed then the murderer just left you to it."

"They're still here. I know they are."

"How can you be so sure?"

"Call it a hunch, call it intuition, but I'm certain. You know I always have these feelings when I'm getting close to figuring out mysteries, and I have it now."

"That's my boy. Max, you'll solve these awful crimes." Mum smiled lovingly, her blind faith in me comforting even though it was unfounded, especially because we were still all trapped here.

"Thanks. And thank you so much for coming. I still can't believe you were out there all night. How did you, er, you know?"

"Go to the toilet?" asked Dad brightly, grinning in a weird way as he turned to Mum.

"Don't you dare!" Mum warned.

"What's going on?" I asked, confused.

"When your mum needed to go, she—"

"You promised never to speak of it again. Oh, the shame." Mum hid her face and for a moment I thought she was crying, but then she lifted her head, defiant, and hissed at Dad, "Do not speak of it! Ever!"

"Stop with the exclamations. You're being way too dramatic. I was just about to tell Max that when you needed to do a number two you—"

"Enough!" Mum jabbed Dad in the arm and he decided that maybe some things were best not shared.

"I think I get the idea," I laughed, my spirits lifting by having them here. One thing I could always rely on them for was to cheer me up. Their unending optimism and positive attitude was why I always tried to look on the bright side of life.

"What now?" asked Mum, changing the subject.

"Yes, can you give us the tour?" asked Dad. "And did I spy toilets? Maybe I can freshen up and finally have a poo."

"So you didn't stick your bum over the side like Mum?" I teased, smiling at Mum who scowled at me then glared at Dad, daring him to confirm things.

"No chance. I have some respect."

"There's a toilet in the back here, so use that. If you don't mind, I'm going outside to have a think. Will you be okay?"

"I'll look after them," said Babs eagerly.

"Thanks, Babs. And it is great to see you both. Thank you for trying to find me. I appreciate it. Do you think Min will have called for help?"

"Course she will have," said Dad. "She'll be going spare because we haven't returned. I bet help will arrive any minute. Don't fret, Son, it will all work out."

"I hope so." The problem was, it hadn't worked out. And I knew that if help did arrive, the chances of this being solved were even less likely. The killer was here, and I needed more time, but I desperately wanted to return to the mainland and escape this place too. What to do? Think. I had to think.

The peace by the harbour was absolute and joyous. Early in the morning like this was always a favourite time of mine, and today was no exception. With only Anxious for company, I was able to truly relax. The little guy was content to be wherever I was, so curled up in my lap and grabbed a nap while I let recent events play out once more.

Blue had been a revelation, but I didn't trust him. I didn't trust any of the residents. What kind of people left visitors stranded without the offer of any assistance whatsoever? They hadn't even come out to see what we were up to, or check we were even alive. Blue had been right about one thing—this was not a place for outsiders.

How could the new Pink be so callous about his brother's demise unless he had something to do with it? How could they be so dismissive of the death, and that of the stranger? Who was that man?

"Mind if I join you?" asked Izzy.

I turned and smiled up at her, then patted the ground beside me and said, "Sure. Be my guest."

Izzy nodded her thanks then settled herself and placed her bag down. She grabbed her notebook and began writing without another word. When she'd finished, she left it on top of her bag like I'd noticed she sometimes did if she thought she'd be making more observations soon.

"Crazy morning, eh?" Izzy smiled weakly, and teased her hair between her fingers, the nails short and bitten. She noticed me staring and said, "A bad habit. I've not done it for ages, but this has been so stressful that I found myself biting them again."

"It's not surprising. How are you holding up? Did you want some space from the others too? I know my folks can be a handful."

"They seem lovely. It's a shame they didn't keep hold of the boat, obviously, but they're sweet."

"Sweet is not a word I'd use to describe them," I chuckled, "but they're good people. The best. They're very scatty, though, and I still can't believe they made it here at all. Dad gets lost going to the bathroom at night in their own home, and I don't think they've ever managed a trip and not got lost."

"I'm the same. I have a terrible sense of direction."

"But you rowed yourself here without any problems?"

"Sure. You can't exactly miss it. It's a massive rock and the only thing for miles."

"Tell that to the pair of fifties freaks inside," I said, smiling.

"Hey, I'm just going to the loo. I'll use the public ones. Won't be a minute."

"Sure thing."

Izzy smiled, then patted Anxious before hurrying off, clearly wanting more privacy than the cafe offered, so I resumed staring out to sea. As I was settling into some much needed alone time, the wind picked up and made me smile as it blew my hair into my face.

A strong gust blew open Izzy's notebook and I grabbed for it before it went into the water, then immediately felt guilty when I realised I was staring at her private thoughts and drawings. Unable to help myself, and checking she wasn't returning, I flipped through the notebook feeling like a terrible person for invading her privacy but keen to understand her better and discover exactly why she was always writing in it.

A few minutes later, and not wanting to risk her discovering me, I closed the book with a deep sigh then continued to stare at the water. The sun warmed my skin and I felt calm, if only for a while.

Chapter 17

When Izzy returned, I said nothing about the book, but she didn't look best pleased when she realised she'd left it out.

"You okay?"

"Sure." Izzy smiled, then sat beside me and picked up her book. "It's precious to me and I shouldn't have left it out of my bag. It might have rained or got knocked into the sea."

"You ever show anyone it?"

She shook her head. "It's private. Nothing special, as I'm not a special person, but it has my thoughts, opinions, and sketches I like to do. I'm not much of an artist, but it makes me happy."

"That's the most important thing. Everyone needs something that brings them joy."

"What makes you happy, Max?"

"Being with this guy." I smiled at Anxious who twitched in his sleep, causing us both to stifle a laugh and lower our voices a little.

"Not just that, surely?"

"Vanlife is awesome, so that is a true pleasure. I told you I used to be a chef, of course, and cooking still brings me immense satisfaction. Min is the most special thing in my life besides Anxious and my folks, so she makes me happy too. What I've also learned is that helping the various communities I come across is very important. Solving the murder mysteries really does help others, and although it's often rather scary and very confusing to see the dark side of people's nature, it's satisfying to know I've helped the families of the deceased or the communities where it happened get some closure."

"Wow, you've got a lot going on."

"Not really. It might not sound like it, but most if the time I'm taking it easy and sitting in my camping chair. I love that chair."

We both burst out laughing as I knew it sounded silly but she understood what I meant. "It's the whole lifestyle, isn't it? You get to travel, always have your home with you, and see lots of cool stuff. It's why I've taken a much-needed break. It's easy to get stuck in a routine and miss out on all the great things this country has to offer, so I decided to do some exploring. It's been good for me. I've loved it. I busk now and then to keep some money coming in, but I've basically had the whole summer off."

"Sounds perfect."

"Mostly it has been. I just wish…"

"What?"

"Nothing. It doesn't matter."

"You can tell me if you want to. I'm good at keeping secrets."

"So am I. Honestly, it was nothing. I think I'll go back inside and see if I can sleep. Max, do you think help will ever arrive? I want off this place. It's creeping me out and I don't like it."

"I'm sure help will come soon enough. But weirdly I don't want to be rescued too soon as I need to solve this mystery first."

"You can't let go of something once you make your mind up, can you?"

"No. Sometimes I think it's a positive trait, other times the opposite. But it's the way I am and I'm at peace with that finally."

"I'm glad. See you later."

I mulled over our conversation and the actions of the people I'd met since I first arrived here, and wondered if this life would ever let me be truly at peace. Just when I thought I was ready for the bad things humans were capable of, I always found myself shocked by what they did. Were any of the people, residents and visitors alike, truly what they seemed, or did everyone have a secret they wanted to remain hidden? I was beginning to suspect they did, and doubted I'd ever uncover the truth behind the facades everyone wore.

I turned when I heard the door open again, and waved at Mum and Dad as they walked over, arm in arm.

"How about that tour you promised?" asked Dad.

"Did I?"

"I think so. Maybe not." Dad shrugged, then added, "Show us around anyway. There must be a lovely view from up the top by the castle. Is it cool?"

"It's pretty cool, yeah. Not large, but a nice old ruin. Come on, I'll show you the way."

I knew better than to comment on Mum's inappropriate footwear, aware that she had climbed a mountain in the exact same shoes. With me in the middle and their arms linked through mine, and Anxious awake and raring to go in a flash, we followed the path away from the cafe and passed the spot where I'd found old Pink. I explained about it as we went, and filled them both in on everything I'd missed out earlier. But I held back the most important part —who the murderer was.

No doubt remained in my mind who the guilty party was, and yet I knew this was far from over. It was one thing to know who it was, and quite another to prove it. For that I would need their help, so although I felt like I was performing an act of subterfuge by not telling them everything, I knew it was for the best in the long run and they would forgive me when the time came. After all, this was my calling, and they agreed on that, so for now we simply walked and chatted, marvelling at the fact they'd managed to make it here in one piece.

I think they found that even more incredible than me.

"Aren't you exhausted?" I asked when we reached the path leading up to the castle. "You haven't slept a wink, have you?"

Dad frowned and said, "How'd you mean? Why wouldn't we have slept?"

"Because you were lost at sea in a tiny rowing boat and could have ended up anywhere and starved or drowned."

"He's such a joker," laughed Mum, adjusting her bandanna and slapping me playfully on the arm.

"A right character at times," agreed Dad.

"Guys, what are you talking about? I'm not joking around."

"Oh, sorry." Dad exchanged a concerned look with Mum, then asked, "Why would we have drowned or died? We knew we'd be alright."

"You weren't concerned?"

"Us?" asked Mum. "No chance. You know what we're like, love. We always get lost. It's our thing. But we knew we'd be fine. It's just the sea, and besides, what was the worst that could have happened?"

"As I said, you could have drowned or starved to death. You didn't even have any water."

"We're optimists. You know that. We figured we'd find you eventually, and we did," said Dad. "I slept like a log. So did your mum."

"Really?"

"Absolutely," said Mum, beaming at me. "We took in turns to rest while the other rowed or looked for lights. It worked out perfectly."

"You guys are incredible." I smiled at my folks, yet again amazed at their upbeat nature and ability to remain positive and confident even under the worst circumstances. "Come on, let's go and see the castle."

With Anxious leading, we made our way slowly up to the top of the island and paused to take in the incredible views it afforded. It really was a beautiful place, and I felt saddened that such a dark stain had tarnished the ground with the blood of two men who were if not innocent then certainly undeserving of such a crime.

"Seems like a fun place to live for a few days, or a short holiday, but I don't get how they can stay here for years," said Dad.

"It's lovely, but I agree. They've all got secrets, that's for sure, and I don't think I'd ever want to live somewhere with any of them as my neighbours. Imagine living somewhere where you didn't get on with anyone. Every time you left the house you'd feel miserable." I couldn't even contemplate such a life, and wondered how much it had affected their mental health. No amount of magical water was worth such a stressful existence.

"Some people can't function in the real world and need to find a different way to live. I understand why they've done it," said Mum, her voice barely a whisper.

"That's very kind, Mum."

"It is what it is, Son. Don't forget, not everyone's as lucky as us. We have each other, and you have Min and Anxious. Other people are alone and struggling to make sense of the world and their place in it. Life is hard, and the modern world is especially difficult to navigate. Computers and all the online nonsense that goes on makes coping almost impossible for so many people and yet they can't find the strength or even realise it's the internet addiction that's causing the problem. These people have found a way to escape all that, so maybe they're not so foolish."

"Wise words, love. Wise words indeed." Dad kissed Mum's cheek and she giggled, their love as apparent as always.

"Really nice sentiment, Mum. You're a very smart, kind woman, and I love you very much." I kissed Mum's other cheek and she beamed, then laughed it off.

"You silly sods. Stop being so soppy or you'll make me cry. One thing I know for sure is I wouldn't want to have to raise children in this day and age. All the mums and dads I've spoken to complain about how hard it is to get their children to go outside and play and stop looking at screens or gaming. It's a complicated world now and I dread to think what the future will be like for the poor kids who don't interact like we did when we were young. Max, I know you had your computer thingy when you were young, but it wasn't like it is now. Now everyone has entertainment at their fingertips whenever they want it and they can't handle being bored. Everyone needs to be bored for at least a while every day. It gives your brain time to rest."

"I totally agree," I said, "but what's brought this on?"

Mum shrugged and said, "This island nonsense got me to thinking. I get it, I really do. People want to escape the world, and you can't blame them for that. Sure, they sound absolutely nutty, but isn't everyone to some degree? I suppose I'm just learning to be more understanding and not judge. Mind you, it is absolutely dumb to live how they do. How do they watch YouTube?"

We laughed and teased each other for a while, back to the usual banter and playfulness that had been a constant as I grew up, and my spirits soared as we fell into the old routines. Mum was right, though, and I wondered what the future held for everyone. Life was certainly more complicated than when they were young, me too, and I was more grateful than ever for choosing a life that allowed me such freedom and an escape from so many of the worries most people had to find a way to cope with every single day.

"Let's have a look around this ruin then," prompted Dad to get me out of my own head.

"Sure thing. Anxious, care to do the honours?"

With a happy bark, the little guy led the way and we followed, exploring the small castle remains and spending quality time together chatting about this and that but staying away from any serious topics.

My folks seemed content to wander around and spend time with us rather than resting, their energy levels much higher than mine, and for a moment I wondered if they'd somehow drunk the water, but reminded myself that this was how they always were. If they weren't busy at home with one project or another, they were off dancing or travelling around and getting lost, enjoying themselves all the while, so I found myself simply having fun for what felt like the first time in ages.

With our mood buoyant, we returned to the bottom of the hill the way we'd gone up then continued around the island, taking our time, watching the birds, enjoying the peace and the warm wind that blew as the sun shone on a beautiful and inspiring day.

Eventually, we made it to the spot where I'd discovered the mystery man, and I explained in detail how we'd found him and what he'd looked like.

"He was up to something here," said Dad, sounding confident.

"What makes you say that?"

"The way he was set up like a scarecrow. To me, that's a warning to someone else, or maybe to all the other residents. Maybe he wasn't even meant to be killed, just left there, but something went wrong."

"What would the killer be warning the others about?"

"Dunno. But this whole water thing is iffy. It has to be about that."

"That's what I thought!" said Mum, wagging a finger at Dad. "Don't steal my ideas."

"I'm not stealing your ideas. I came up with it first."

"Did not!" Mum pouted and added, "I thought it ages ago."

"Guys, that doesn't matter. What about the water?"

"It stands to reason that this dead guy was a warning as he was set out in the path for a local or a tourist to find. Then they'd know not to do whatever they had planned. I bet one of them was going to meet this guy and see about bottling and selling the water or trying to figure out how to get it for themselves and cut the others off. Something like that anyway."

"That's what I was thinking too," said Mum with another glare at Dad, which he managed to duck away from just in time before he was incinerated.

"So you really think it's about the water?"

"Yes," they both agreed, looking smug and as though they'd solved the whole thing.

"Maybe it does," I mused, trying to decipher how the pieces fit together with what I was already sure I knew. "Maybe news of it has leaked somehow and the killer was meeting the stranger and things went wrong. Or maybe he tried to get more information about it and the killer didn't want them to so ended up using him as an example to the others. There's a lot to still figure out with this, and it doesn't explain why the old Pink was murdered."

"That's easy," crowed Dad.

"I thought the same thing," said Mum hurriedly. "Whatever your father says, I thought it first."

"Did not!" snapped Dad.

"Did too." Mum crossed her arms; conversation over.

"As I was saying," Dad paused to blow Mum a kiss, showing there were no hard feelings, and she caught it with a smile then slapped it to her lips, "it's easy to figure out why this Pink fellow was killed and in the way he was."

"I'm all ears," I blurted, truly intrigued to hear what he thought.

"He was obviously a bully and got what he deserved." Dad smiled at us, smug, but Mum hissed at him. "What?"

"That is absolutely not what I was thinking. You are such a pilchard."

"I am not. And I already told you lots of times to stop stealing my sayings. I say pilchard, not you."

"Pilchard."

"Mum, what's your take on this?"

"The way you described how Pink was killed, it was for the same reason as the other man. To make a point. To either show the islanders that they better toe the line, or Pink did something so insulting to the killer that they didn't just want to stab him, they wanted to humiliate them. This was personal, not just to stop them doing something the murderer might not have agreed with."

"And what do you both think about the symbols carved into them? Why do that? Any ideas what they mean?"

"To me it looked like the work of a maniac. Deranged if you ask me," said Dad.

"That's what I thought too." Mum held a finger up to Dad before he started arguing with her and he decided silence was the best option.

"And now let's get to the real question. Who do you think did it?"

"Babs!" hissed Mum.

"White!" shouted Dad.

They looked at each other, astonished by the other's suggestion.

"No way was it Babs," chortled Dad, shaking his head.

"It was. It wasn't White, I'm sure of that," growled Mum.

"Why Babs?" I asked, surprised by her insistence.

"We've been chatting a lot and I think she's cagey. Nice, and she's certainly a new friend, but she's the artsy type and the symbols are probably something she's seen in a book or something and fancied a go on real flesh. Don't forget, she's a mortician, so knows her way around a body. She did it. She knew about the water, I bet, and wanted in on the action so brought the mystery fella here in secret, or maybe with Bob, to test it or something. Then once he told her about it she did the deed. I bet Pink found out what she was up to and he had to go too."

"What a load of rubbish!" said Dad with a belly laugh. "You've got it all wrong. The only possible explanation is that it was White so he could get the guy's house or his stuff but it backfired. Max said it himself that White was right there pretending he hadn't seen Pink when I bet he did it then got disturbed by Max so pretended he'd never seen the dead guy. No way could you miss someone dead right by you."

"It's certainly possible," I conceded, "but neither of you are right."

My parents studied me in silence, then both smiled as their eyes widened and they both cheered, "You already know who did it, don't you?"

"I do, but I have no idea why," I admitted. "We need to figure that out so we can prove it was them."

"And you have a cunning plan, don't you?" said Mum, brimming with pride.

"I might have an idea that should work."

"But only with our help, right?" asked Dad, unable to hide his enthusiasm.

"Exactly. Now, here's what I was thinking, but we need to go and do it now, as I'm sure a rescue party must be on its way. Min will be worried sick, and no way will she rest until we're found."

"Then let's get to it!" cheered Mum.

Chapter 18

We returned to the harbour to find everyone gathered outside the cafe where they'd brought out several chairs so they could remain together but be comfortable. Everyone was subdued and seemed rather moody, with nobody talking.

"Anything wrong?" asked Dad in his usual blunt manner, although I was surprised he even picked up on the vibe as he was rarely good at reading people, just like Mum.

"Why do you all have faces like a monkey's bum?" asked Mum.

"What does that even mean?" hissed Carl, glancing up.

"Red and angry looking," Mum explained cheerily, ignoring Carl's tone.

"Are monkey bums angry looking?" asked Babs, reaching for a bottle of wine and unscrewing the cap then taking a big hit before passing it to Bob who did the same.

"Course they are. You would be if your bottom was always on display." Mum grinned at her captive audience and to be fair they had perked up, mouths twitching with amusement and still a little shock at the woman stood before them in high heels, a polka dot dress, and seemingly unaffected by her boat-based ordeal.

"Fancy a vino, love?" asked Dad with a wink.

"It's very early, isn't it?" asked Mum, having absolutely no idea what the time was.

"Babs and Bob are drinking, so it must be five o'clock somewhere," said Dad.

"Then yes! That would be lovely."

"Right you are. Um, where's the booze stash, Babs?"

Babs told him, so Dad hurried inside then returned a moment later with a few bottles and set them down on the table then poured a glass for Mum.

"My lady always drinks from a glass," he explained to everyone.

"Thanks, love." Mum took a sip, smiled, and said, "Yum. Lovely. So, what's up, everyone? Why the long faces?"

"Because we're stuck on the island!" snapped Carl, causing Mum and Dad to whirl on him.

"Don't you talk to my wife like that. She's a lady and deserves to be treated with respect."

"Watch your tone, Carl," I said in a much calmer manner. "I know everyone's stressed and wants to go home, but that doesn't mean it's okay to be rude."

"That's okay," said Mum. "I'm sure Carl is going to apologise and be nice from now on. Aren't you, Carl?" Mum seemed to grow a foot and loomed over the seated Carl who looked from me to Dad, then to Mum, and nodded.

"Sorry to be rude. I'm just tired and Max is right. I want off this rock and to go home. Maybe not home, but at least to the campsite so I can relax and not worry about being murdered."

"Unless it was you who killed them and you can't wait to get away from the scene of your crime," said Mum, daring him to contradict her.

"You what!?" demanded Carl as he shoved his chair back and jumped to his feet.

"All I'm saying is that maybe you're the killer." Mum was utterly calm as Carl shook his head, his long hair hiding his red face as he stammered.

"You're nuts. This woman is crazy. Why would you say such a thing? I didn't kill anyone. Why would I?"

"You look like a killer," said Dad, coming to Mum's rescue. "Sketchy features, long hair, and all in black. You're a right moody one, aren't you? Classic killer look if you ask me."

"Nobody did ask you," hissed Carl. "And besides, we all know who the artistic one is around here." Carl spun and pointed at Izzy who was merrily scribbling in her notebook, a wry smile on her face.

When everyone stopped talking, she raised her head, and her smile faded as she asked, "Me?" with a short laugh. "You're saying I killed those two men and carved their flesh?"

"Well, um, no, but I was just saying that I'm not the only one who should be a suspect."

"That's right," said Mum merrily. "It could just as easily have been Bob. Or maybe he and Babs are in this together. It makes sense, what with them being in the death business already."

"Makes total sense, love," agreed Dad, upending his wine then staring at the empty bottle in accusation. "Hey, where'd my wine go?"

"You drank it, you pilchard."

"I am not a pilchard!"

"Shut up! Just shut up!" warned Bob. "We are not killers, and would never do such a thing. But Jill is right about one thing. Those carvings were very well done, and that means it's someone with a very steady hand and a keen eye for detail."

"And zero qualms about cutting up a human being," added Babs with a smile for her husband.

Once again, all focus turned to Izzy, who, yet again, was making notes. This time she snapped her book closed, face like thunder, and hissed, "Don't you dare accuse me again. It's obviously one of the residents. Who else could it be?

And why would I, or any of us, even dream of killing those men?"

"Why don't you hazard a guess?" I suggested, watching how she reacted but keeping a keen eye on the others who were now at their wits' end. Exhausted, stressed, drunk in two cases, and hungry. Everyone was liable to let something slip, and I knew this was now or never if we were to get to the bottom of this before we were rescued.

"I wouldn't know where to begin. How could I?"

"Mum and Dad had an interesting theory. They think maybe it's to do with the water. That the residents want to keep it secret is something we know now, but what if someone else knew about it and wanted to cash in on this strange water? Maybe bottle and sell it?"

"I'm not following." Izzy gnawed at a fingernail already chewed down to the quick as she frowned.

"Maybe this person who discovered the water's power and that they could make a fortune got found out by Pink and he threatened them. Maybe they killed him to stop him from attacking them, or maybe just to keep him quiet."

"It's a theory, sure."

"Max, what are you getting at here?" asked Carl. "Can we please stop talking about this? I just want to forget any of this ever happened. It's too much, and you're freaking Izzy out now. Izzy, I'm sorry I said what I did. I was lashing out and I wish I hadn't."

"It's fine. We're all stressed and tired."

"Maybe the mystery man was involved too. Partners with the killer. Someone who could help get the water bottled. What if the killer fell out with them when they discovered they'd killed Pink?"

"It's not about the water!" yelled Izzy, looking close to tears as she stared at her finger and the blood from her biting. She sucked it then let her hand drop.

I kept a very close eye on Anxious while this was happening, and noted how he'd moved to the empty ground between me and my folks and the others. He was focused on Izzy, with his head cocked and ears flat, meaning he was confused, but thinking things through in his own special way.

"How would you know that, Izzy? How could you possibly know?"

"Because it sounds dumb. Max, it's just a theory, and we've done nothing but come up with increasingly lame reasons why those men were murdered, but none of us truly knows and I don't think we ever will."

"That's where you're wrong, Izzy," I whispered. "I know, and so do you."

"What are you talking about? Max, get some rest. It's been a trying time and you're overwhelmed. Sit down and relax. I can't believe you're accusing me of something. You are, aren't you? I thought we were friends?"

"So did I. I wish this weren't true, but it is. Why did you do it, Izzy?"

"You aren't joking?" Carl parted his hair and turned to Izzy to ask, "You did this?"

"Of course not! Don't be ridiculous."

"It's a poor show to be accusing the girl like that, Max," grumbled Bob. "She's a great gal."

"We're a team," slurred Babs, almost keeling over sideways in her chair before Bob grabbed her. "Izzy's one of us. She's right and you're just exhausted. Stop being so silly."

I took a step forward, crouched beside my best buddy, and waved a biscuit in front of his face then said, "Anxious, fetch the book."

It was a trick we'd learned years ago when he was little and being shown how to sit or roll over and a few other things, and he always enjoyed games of fetch. It allowed me to teach him the words for quite a few objects.

With a quick turn of the head to check I was serious, and I nodded that I was, Anxious leapt from his seated position and snatched the book from Izzy's lap before she had a chance to react.

"Hey!" Izzy was out of her chair instantly, but Anxious had already turned and raced back to me then dropped the book, eyes glued to my hand.

I grabbed it, gave him the treat, then backed away to get some space before Izzy could try to retrieve it.

With a nod to my folks, they closed ranks, and with Anxious having already inhaled his treat he stood in front of them, growling a warning at Izzy who stopped dead in her tracks, flustered and looking ready to either cry or run. Possibly both.

Everyone was standing now, shouting their opinions, insisting I was out of order and should give Izzy her book back. When Izzy stepped forward again and Anxious upped his warning by growling and baring his teeth, she backed up and everyone stilled.

"I'm sorry, everyone, but don't you want to know for sure one way or the other?" There were murmurs of agreement, so I continued. "I got a quick look at Izzy's notebook and found something very interesting. I didn't have time to read much, but something really caught my eye."

"Give it back, Max." Izzy's words were barely a whisper, and she sounded defeated, but there was a slyness to her eyes and although I found it hard, I knew I had to continue.

"I'm sorry, but I can't."

"It's mine. Private. Like a diary. You can't read it. I haven't done anything wrong."

"Then how do you explain this?" I flipped through the pages until I came to the one I'd seen earlier, then held the book up for all to see. "It's the motif carved into the two men. See?"

Everyone crowded around apart from Izzy, who slumped into the nearest chair, gnawing frantically on her nails.

"So she drew the symbol." Carl shrugged, like it wasn't important. "She's been doing lots of drawing and writing. It's no big deal."

"He's right," agreed Bob. "Just because she saw the bodies and drew the carving doesn't mean she's the killer. You've gone too far, Max."

"You listen to my son," demanded Mum. "None of you are understanding."

"Thanks, Mum. And sure, if she'd copied the symbol off the bodies it would mean nothing, but this was drawn weeks before any of this happened. She's written about the design and if I go back a few pages we can see different variations of it. It predates the killing by weeks. Unless she can explain how her design came to be carved on Pink and the other man, it's proof she was the one who killed them. I haven't had time to read the notebook, but I'm sure there will be a lot more to prove her guilt."

"No way!" gasped Carl, turning with the others to confront Izzy. "You didn't, did you? How do you explain this, Izzy? Did you know them both?"

"Of course I didn't know them!"

"You may not have known them," I said, "but you met Pink at some point, didn't you? Something happened and you wanted revenge. As to the other man, he's still a mystery. I think he simply saw what you did and you murdered him too. Who was he?"

"That's what I had to find out," mumbled Izzy, eyes downcast, staring at her ruined fingers. She wiped the blood on her dress then looked up, eyes red and puffy but determined.

"So it was you?" gasped Carl, his anger flaring for a brief moment before his shoulders sagged and he pushed past the others to sit beside Izzy. "Why? You had your whole future ahead of you. You killed two men and did despicable things to them, and for what?"

"It's complicated." Izzy's eyes darted constantly, but then she sighed and slumped back, folded her hands in her lap as if she had finally found peace, and let her head hang.

"You can tell us," soothed Carl. "We deserve to know."

Izzy's eyes snapped open and she asked, "Why? Why should I tell any of you anything?"

"We're your friends. We looked out for each other through this. The boats sinking, the weird residents, all this water business. Was it about the water? Are Jack and Jill right? Did you want to sell it or something? Get rich?"

"It has nothing to do with the water!" Izzy screamed, her face turning puce, but she didn't stand, and she refused to meet Carl's eyes.

"I never even thought about the boats," gasped Carl. "Izzy, you stole the oars, sank the boats, and ruined the wiring on the speedboat? Why? That makes no sense."

"It does actually," I said. "Once Izzy killed the men, she knew they'd be discovered and there weren't that many people who could be blamed for it. Obviously, suspicion would fall on the residents, but if we left the moment one body was found maybe the other wouldn't be for a while. It was better if we were stranded. It stopped us looking like suspects."

"That can't be right, surely?" asked Mum. "She could have done it then got away. You all could have. You'd tell the police, they'd ask you a few questions, then you'd all be about your business. Instead, she made sure you were stuck here. I don't get it."

"Mum, it was so she seemed innocent."

Our attention turned to Izzy, who was squirming in her seat and wringing her hands. "After I killed Pink, I saw the other man watching me. He ran off. I panicked, didn't know what to do, so returned to the harbour. I couldn't believe my luck, as the boats were obviously damaged. The speedboat had the wires pulled out and the rowing boats were filling with water. Not that any of you idiots noticed."

"You swear you didn't ruin the boats? Truly?" asked Babs.

"Yes! Why won't you believe me?"

"You murdered two men! Why would we believe what you say?" asked Babs, shaking her head and wiping a tear. "You're such a lovely girl too."

"I liked you," said Carl. "We got on well and you seemed really nice. You did this, but why? Why kill Pink? This is what it's been about, right?"

"Of course it is."

"What about the symbols on those poor men?" asked Dad. "Why go to such extremes, love? That was a terrible thing to do. It's not normal."

"You don't understand. None of you do."

"Wait, just so I'm clear about this," said Mum. "This has nothing to do with the water?"

"No! Who cares about the stupid water?" screamed Izzy. "I had no idea about it until I found the stranger. He begged to be given some before I killed him, and I got him to tell me all about it. I wasn't sure I believed him until I found Max laying in the sea, unconscious."

"You saved me and wrote the warning," I said. "I recognised the handwriting from your notebook. Izzy, why did you rescue me?"

"There'd been enough death already. I saw you covering Pink's body, which was thoughtful, and I just knew you were a nice person."

"You killed Pink and tortured a stranger. Those aren't exactly the actions of a kind person."

"That was different. I had to protect myself, so had no choice but to eliminate that weird bloke. And as for Pink." Izzy actually spat on the ground, which everyone found more shocking than anything else, and gasped as we stood back in a semi-circle to hear the rest of Izzy's sorry tale.

"You may as well tell us," I said. "Thank you for saving me. I truly appreciate that, but to commit such barbarism is shocking. Izzy, how could you? Why?"

"You know I'm a mime artist," she began, which caused everyone to swallow and take another step back for fear she would suddenly jump up and perform her act. Now most certainly wasn't the time for such things.

"No need to show us," blurted Carl.

"Don't worry, I won't. Look, I understand it's not for everyone, and that's cool. I met that Pink guy in town the other day. I guess he'd gone for supplies. I was busking to earn a little cash, and it was going well, but he spoiled it. He made fun of me right in front of everyone. Laughed and teased me and ridiculed my new sign."

"The symbol on his back?" I asked.

"Yes. He said it was dumb and I was dumb, and I looked ridiculous. I'm used to being teased, but this was different. Cruel almost. I took a lot of time designing my new logo for my posters and he made me feel so small and useless. I took a trip to the island not knowing he lived here, but when we met each other he recognised me and kept teasing me as I was walking past where he was fishing. I shouted at him, but he ran after me with his fishing gear and tripped. The hook stuck in him and it tangled around his throat. I saw red and pulled it tight until he died, then I must have gone rather crazy and I stripped him and carved the symbol into him. Not exactly the same as my new logo, but a circle and a stylised hand. Showing I'd never be teased again."

"Izzy, you really need some serious help," said Carl. "And you got seen by this other guy, whoever he was?"

"Yes, but he ran off. I chased after him and found him, then you know the rest. I did wrong, I know that, but he made fun of my passion. Mime is an art form and he belittled it and me. I lost the plot and don't even remember half of what I did." Izzy was done, and stared at her hands. "Can I have my book back?" she asked, glancing up.

"I'm sorry, but you can't. The police will want it. Come on, it's time to go. I can hear a boat. Everyone get ready to leave."

We turned to see several RNLI boats approaching at high speed before they slowed when close to the island.

Salvation was finally here, but for one of us it would be nothing but swapping one prison for an even smaller one, with no hope of escape.

Chapter 19

"Anxious, guard Izzy please."

He nodded, then stood tall and proud, eyes fixed on her.

Izzy met my gaze and said, "Don't worry, I'm not going anywhere. It's over. In a way, I'm glad."

"You are?"

"I think I need help. I don't know what happened to me, but this isn't who I am. Years of pent-up frustration bubbled over and I couldn't stop myself. Now it's done. Go and tell them. It's for the best."

I asked everyone to wait for a few minutes while I hurried over to the men and women already securing the two boats. A solid man with a buzzcut and strong arms was securing the rope then calling orders to the crew, so I approached then waited until he turned to me.

"There's a killer mime artist with us and she's just admitted double murder. We need to call the police. Do you have a radio to get in touch with them? There's no phone signal here."

"Doesn't surprise me," he grunted, his lip twitching, but otherwise no emotion showed on his tanned face. "Mimes are not to be trusted. Makes me shudder just thinking about them pulling those faces when they pretend to be stuck in invisible boxes." He did genuinely shudder, and so did I, as it was true, although his attitude was rather shocking.

"How did you know to come and rescue us? And thank you, by the way. It's been a very trying experience."

"We got a call from a woman. Min, her name was. Are you Max?"

"Yes, that's me."

"Right. Makes sense. She said you were here and that because you hadn't returned it most likely meant there was a murder. Everyone thought she was nuts and laughed it off, but we came as there were reports about a few tourists not returning and John who runs the boat rental business has been going spare about not getting his boats back. Sorry it took so long, but we had an emergency out in the channel and it took all night, then one of the boats had engine issues so we've been fixing that. But here we are."

"That's great! Not about the trouble you had, but that you're here now. We have two bodies stored in the back of the cafe. The locals have been no help at all. We need to get out of here. Everyone's dehydrated, exhausted, and hungry, and a few have been drinking, so watch out for Babs and Bob."

"Don't worry, I know all about the residents. Everyone around here does. Bunch of mad old fools who think there's something special in the water."

"You know about that?"

"Sure. We get people trying to get to the island all the time. Some even swim, saying it's part of the ritual cleansing to be accepted. Load of nonsense, obviously, but over the years it's led to quite a few deaths. My advice is to stay clear and never come back. Who got killed?"

"A big guy who was called Pink, although his brother is here now and has taken the name, and a stranger. Nobody knows who he is, but Izzy, she's the mime artist, said he had been hiding out here for a while trying to get pally with the locals."

"I'll call it in right away. You best get on the other boat with everyone else who wants to leave, and we'll wait with this Izzy until the police come. Give me your details so I can let you know if you're needed, but once back at shore you'll have to explain everything properly to the police. They'll most likely be waiting. I'm Tony, by the way."

"Nice to meet you, Tony." We shook, and I gave him my number, then went to explain to everyone.

Ten minutes later, we were speeding across the sea and heading back to the mainland. We passed a police boat when we'd almost reached shore, and I could see scores of officers lining the harbour where we were to disembark. I checked my phone repeatedly, then called Min to let her know we were on our way the moment I got a signal. The sound of her voice was beautiful.

Even though everyone was utterly fried, we had to answer endless questions about what had happened since we'd arrived on the island the day before, which took forever. Detectives wanted all the details before they headed over to investigate, so I told them everything, going over how the men had been found, how we moved them, how I realised it was Izzy, and even about my folks arriving and their nighttime adventure.

Every so often I could hear Mum and Dad as they gave their statements, the officer in charge of them stepping back and cutting short the interview before they began extolling the virtues of all things fifties and stopping him from doing his job. The others looked tired enough to collapse, and the officers clearly understood this and eventually let us sit at a cafe they'd cleared out so we could get some refreshments and recover before going our separate ways.

"So it's over," sighed Carl, gulping his coffee.

"For us. Not for Izzy," lamented Dad with a sigh. "Poor woman lost her mind. A word of warning to you all. Never take up mime. It'll be the death of either you or some poor sucker."

Everyone agreed they would never dream of doing such a thing, and then we fell into silence as we watched the detectives board a boat with several more officers then chase across the water, disturbing the protesting gulls, but delighting the small crowd that had gathered to find out what was going on.

"So, it was nothing to do with the water?" asked Mum, applying fresh lipstick and checking herself in a compact from her bag.

"Nothing at all, Mum. Just a woman who got pushed too close to the edge then fell into a dark place."

"And you solved another mystery!" crowed Dad, slapping my back and grinning.

"Barely. It was only because I saw the drawing in her notebook."

"Max, come on, be truthful. No need to act so coy. You already suspected her, didn't you?"

"I did," I admitted.

"Why?"

"A few little things she said and did. I thought early on that she'd saved me from the water when I blacked out as who else had a pen and paper handy? I wasn't sure why she kept quiet about it, which made me suspect there was something else going on."

"I never would have thought of that!" said Bob. "Smart. What else?"

"She was the first one here, and knew the place too well even though she said she'd never been before. She had, but pretended she hadn't because she didn't want to make herself a suspect. Sometimes she did things without checking, like knew where everything was in the cafe or when we walked about. She'd come before looking for Pink, I bet, then tried again yesterday and found him. I told the police that, so I'm sure they'll be asking her."

"So it was premeditated?" asked Carl.

"Maybe, or maybe not. Maybe she was just angry and wanted to have it out with him, but when he got tangled in his fishing line she took advantage and got the revenge she craved. She'll get help, but maybe it's too late for her now. She'll never be let out of jail."

"Maybe she will at some point," said Dad. "That's not your problem, Son. You did good and stopped her hurting anyone else. Never trust a mime."

Everyone agreed with him, so we finished our drinks and said a rather sorrowful goodbye to each other. We'd bonded, that was for sure, and each promised to get in touch on occasion, then it was just me and my folks and one utterly exhausted Jack Russell asleep in my arms.

My phone sprang into life and rang, so I fished it out and my heart beat fast as I saw the caller's name. "Min!"

"Turn around," she said.

I did as she asked and smiled as she waved from the path leading from the top of the village. "Wait there, or let me know where you're parked. A little privacy would be great about now." I glanced at Mum and Dad who were inside the cafe ordering more drinks and food.

"Are you okay? I was so worried."

"Fine now. Where are you parked?"

Min gave directions so I rushed inside, told my parents to enjoy their food and then give me a call, then hurried off, a bounce in my step, because the woman I adored was here and I'd made it through another adventure relatively unscathed.

Chapter 20

"I can't even begin to tell you how pleased I am to see you," I gasped, my arms spread wide as I stumbled forward, knowing I had a cheesy grin on my face.

"Do you mean me or Vee?" giggled Min, nodding to Vee beside her, gleaming in the midday sun like a goddess almost as magnificent as her.

"Both," I laughed, staggering, then falling forward into the love of my life's arms. I could have stayed there for eternity, wrapped in her embrace, sniffing her hair, taking in her essence.

"Max?"

"Mmm?"

"Are you sniffing my hair right now? You know that's weird, right?"

"I am not. And even if I was, it isn't weird."

"You carry on," she soothed, stifling a titter. "By the looks of you, I think you deserve it. Have you seen your folks? They went off to find you last night and didn't come back. I've been so worried. When you didn't meet me, I was cross, but then upset, and when they arrived they kept freaking me out talking about drowning. They left in a boat and I haven't seen them since. What if they're dead?"

"They're not dead," I mumbled into her sweet-smelling hair, my nostrils filled with the essence of pear, apple blossom, and general Min deliciousness.

Min eased me back and held my hands at arm's length, then asked, "How do you know?"

"Because I saw them a minute ago. They're getting some food. They made it to the island, but… Don't worry about it for now. It's a long story, but they're safe. They're most likely bending the lifeguard's ear about how he should steer his boat and generally being a nuisance. They should be here soon."

"That's a relief. Max, what happened? Oh, sorry, Anxious." We smiled as he pawed at her legs, desperate for a cuddle, so she picked him up and made a massive fuss of him while he squirmed with pleasure before rolling over, tongue lolling, tail hanging between her arms as she tickled his tummy and laughed.

"It's so nice to see you happy," I said, meaning every word. "Min, I missed you so much and worried I might never see you again. It's been awful on the island, and things got more and more crazy. Never, ever go there," I warned.

"Okay," she said with a frown. "What happened?"

"Later, okay? First, I need to sit down, and I'm dying for a cuppa in my own mug. A strong coffee would do the trick. But I also want to say hello to Vee. I missed her so much too. Is that dumb?"

"Not at all. We've been spending a lot of time together since I arrived. When you weren't here, I decided to go off and explore. We had great fun. I figured you just lost track of time until the evening, then I began to worry."

"So you both got on without us?" I asked with a wink.

"We sure did. Vee behaved really well, and I got the hang of driving her. We even did a hill start."

"I'm impressed." And I was, as I still struggled with the finer aspects of handling a 67 VW with what sometimes felt like a mind of her own.

"You should be. I slept in her alone last night, which was odd, and I missed you, but we managed. I sat out for a while with Jack and Jill before they went to their hotel, but then they turned back up and said they were going to go and find you. I warned them not to as it was getting dark, but they promised they'd just nip to the island as the man said it was only twenty minutes, but never returned. Then I had to get the coastguard involved when I realised they were probably in trouble too. I don't know what I was thinking letting them go. They have zero sense of direction. It's been so stressful."

"Thanks for calling them and thanks for looking out for us. I'm surprised it took the coastguard so long to reach us though."

"Not as surprised as they were. Someone nobbled their boat and it took hours before they could get a replacement."

"Wait! Someone nobbled their boat?"

"Yes, why? Max, what's going on?"

"What's going on is I thought I had this thing solved and wrapped up nicely. But it seems this isn't over yet. Min, let's grab a seat and get that coffee. I need to discuss something with you, explain a few things, and see what you think."

"This is another murder mystery, isn't it? Who were those people on the boat? There are a lot of police around too."

"They're the other tourists from the island. It's a long story and isn't over yet, but they're going back to their campsites as they're exhausted. I guess I'll have to talk to the police again, especially now, but first let's have that coffee."

Vee was parked in a small car park overlooking the quaint harbour, so we wandered over, arm in arm, with Anxious yawning as he skipped off ahead, keen to see Vee too. He greeted her in a way I would never dream of, and when he'd finished cocking his leg against the wheel, he sat and waited while Min opened the side door then jumped in and immediately curled up on the bench seat and closed his eyes with a satisfied groan. For him the adventure was over, for me, maybe not so much.

Min beamed at me as she stepped inside then put the kettle on to boil, and I couldn't resist having a wander around my classic beauty, the other love of my life. It was astonishing how much I'd missed her after one night away, and I wanted to walk around her and admire the lines, the shape, the classic look of this retro vehicle, and enjoy the splash of bright orange and white two-tone paint job that still looked incredible after so many years.

Halfway along the driver's side, I paused, shocked by what I saw. For a moment I felt lightheaded and feared I'd drunk the magic water by mistake, but shook it off and closed then opened my eyes, believing it must have been a dream.

It wasn't.

It was still there.

What was the meaning of this? Was it Min? Was she giving Vee a new paint job? Surely not. Vandals? It was a strange thing to do if it was. It was actually very cool, but it made no sense and I was annoyed as hell that someone had taken it upon themselves to do such a thing without my permission. Unless it really was Min.

"Min, can you come here for a moment?" I called.

"Just a minute. The kettle's about to boil."

I waited while she sorted out the coffee, then stood back when she came around to my side.

"Here you go." Min handed me a steaming mug of the good stuff and I took a sip even though it was scalding, as that's how keen I was to get some caffeine in me.

"Thanks. Boy, I needed this. Um, what do you know about this?" I nodded to the side of Vee and watched as Min's eyes went wide in shock.

"I… How? When? Max, I've never seen this before. How could it have happened? I haven't been here that long, and I didn't even notice it when I got in earlier at the campsite. Mind you, I was preoccupied, but surely I would have seen it?" Min stepped forward, then reached out to touch the new partial paint job that was over the driver's door and a little on the side panel beneath the window. "It's dry."

"Spray paint dries quickly. What do you think it means?"

"I have no idea. None at all. The colours are nice, and it doesn't make Vee look bad or anything. Maybe it was kids doing a random design. Oh, gosh," Min's hand shot to her mouth, "you don't think it's anything to do with what's happened, do you? What did happen?"

"I'll tell you in a minute once we sit down, but no, I can't see that this is related. It's pretty, and weirdly I think I like it, but it's not cool someone's spray-painting our home."

"Our home?" Min's eyebrows reached for the sky as she smiled, her tanned face beautiful as always, and I couldn't take my eyes off her as she brushed golden hair from her face.

"You know what I mean," I laughed. "I wonder who did this?"

"No idea, and I suppose it could have been done at any time. What do you think it means? They clearly didn't finish the job."

"I'm not sure. I like the curves and the colours. It's almost like a tag. Graffiti artists call them tags when they write their names."

"I know what a tag is! I guess now we'll never know."

We stood back to get a better look at the impromptu art, and I had to admit that whoever did it was skilled with a spray can. The outline was in black, with white accents to make the image three-dimensional, but it was like they hadn't quite finished what they were doing and had hardly begun their work before changing their mind. With the infill of the design in a pale turquoise, it offset the retro orange and the off-white of the original paint job quite well, and somehow, and I wasn't sure exactly how, it worked.

"I think it's cool!" I declared, sipping my coffee.

"Me too. Should we keep it?"

"We'll have to, at least for a while. Otherwise it's a total respray and that will cost a lot. Anyway, right now there are other things going on. Let's sit down and I'll explain everything."

"I'm just glad you're back safe and sound." Min stood on tiptoe, I bent at the knee, and our lips met.

Suddenly, life felt perfect.

We returned to the other side and checked in on Anxious who was sleeping soundly, so we settled in the camping chairs and I couldn't help grinning despite the exhaustion and the weird way I felt.

"What's so funny?"

"Just how amazing it feels to sit in this slightly uncomfortable chair. I missed it. I like it."

"You're weird. You do know that, right? Chasing down to Cornwall to catch the last few days of warm weather. Still wearing Crocs and your cut-offs and a vest. It's not summer now."

"It is as far as I'm concerned. If the sun's out and it's warm it's summer no matter what anyone else says. And look at you. Short shorts to show off your tan, a pink vest, and don't tell me you haven't been sitting out in the sun whenever you get the chance. You've got a better tan than ever."

Min stretched out her beautiful legs and I tried to hide my gulp, but knew I was staring.

"I may have got the being-outside-no-matter-what bug," she laughed, noting where my eyes lingered but just wiggling her red-painted toes and grinning at me.

Things were getting better and better by the minute.

We drank our coffee while I recounted our adventure, Min taking it in her stride although becoming increasingly incredulous as the tale continued. When I'd finished, she said nothing, just knelt before me and hugged me tight.

"Thank you. I needed that more than I could have ever explained."

"I know." Min stroked my hair and I fell asleep right there, as happy as I'd ever been in my entire life.

The sleep may not have been long—I was still too amped to truly relax—but when I woke up half an hour later, Min was still there, still stroking my hair, and smiling at me.

"I love you," I murmured as I opened my eyes.

"I know. And I love you too. The kettle's about to boil. Do you want another coffee? I know I haven't had a crazy adventure like you, but I didn't get a wink of sleep so am exhausted."

"Coffee would be great. I'm sorry that you worried, and I honestly tried my best to get back, but it wasn't possible."

"I think you need to tell me the rest. You dropped off before you could finish. Is that okay?"

"I will. I promise. But can we have the coffee first?"

With a sympathetic smile, Min made the coffee, and it tasted better than the first now I'd relaxed. With a sigh, I continued to recount the whole sorry tale.

"Max, that sounds... Incredible! Utterly bonkers. The residents were really like that? You aren't exaggerating?"

"If anything I think I played down how strange they were. Apparently, it's been that way for years. They refuse to talk to each other, keep to themselves, but there's been this tradition with the water every week for as long as anyone can remember. It means they never want to leave. They become addicted to it, and it's almost a religion. Maybe it is a religion. Anyway, that's my story. I assumed I had this figured out, but now I realise there's something else I need to do. I thought Izzy was just being awkward by not explaining about the boats, but something you said earlier made me realise she was telling the truth, at least about one thing."

Anxious yawned as he made an appearance at the open door then hopped down and wandered over to us, his tail whipping around like he was preparing to be airborne, then jumped into Min's lap and almost purred as she stroked him.

"He's pleased to see you. We both missed you."

"I missed you guys too. What now?"

"Now I have this one loose end to tie up, then this thing is done once and for all. I know it doesn't really matter, as we have the killer, but I hate not knowing the full picture. Plus, I want to be sure I'm right. Can you wait here? I won't be long?"

"Sure. Be safe. Take Anxious with you."

"Don't worry about me, and I'm definitely taking the wonder dog."

Anxious looked up at me as I spoke, then barked in agreement.

"Yes, you really are a wonder dog," I laughed. "Meaning, sometimes I wonder if you're a dog at all, or more like my guardian angel."

"Max, what really happened on that island? You're sounding strange with talk of angels and that other stuff. Is it true? Are you missing something out?"

I pondered the question for a moment as I scratched my chin, then answered truthfully, "I honestly don't know. What I know for sure is there was definitely something in the water." With a smile and a wave, I went to put the final piece of the puzzle in its rightful place.

Chapter 21

It was a relatively short walk back to the small shack where I'd rented the boat from. As I approached, I spied John bent over a rowing boat, a variety of tools beside him on a portable workbench. With the small vessel upside down, it was impossible to miss the hole in the bottom, and I wondered how he'd managed to get it back here.

Was I right about this? Or was I still a little trippy from the magic water I'd consumed that had almost killed me? I liked to think I was of sound mind, but when I began giggling and had to duck out of sight until it subsided, I wasn't so sure. Checking myself over, I became certain I was okay. It was just the comedown after the adrenaline and the sheer madness of what had occurred, but my head was clear and in no small part that was thanks to knowing Min was safe and that she'd done all she could to help us.

"Hi, remember us?" I asked as John stood and stretched out his back. For a man in his mid-thirties, he looked good, the tan and wiry muscles from working on boats all day no doubt keeping him in shape.

John rubbed at his stubble, then ran his fingers through an unruly mop of blond surfer-dude hair and grinned. "Sure I do. Max, right?"

"That's right," I said amiably. "Although, I think we both know it isn't usual for you to remember the names of people you rent rowing boats to for a few hours."

"Maybe you're the exception," he laughed, eyes roaming.

"Or maybe you knew who I was and decided to give things a little push?" I suggested.

"I'm not sure I'm following." John reached for a mug of what looked like tea, took a sip, then placed it back down and asked, "What can I do for you? Sorry about what happened. It sounds awful. I've spoken to the police and had to answer a ton of questions, but at least they let me go and recover the boats. I've only got one so far, but I'll go back out later and get the rest. It's a bit of a squeeze on the island right now, but I wanted to make a start on the repairs. I won't earn any money unless I get them up and running soon."

"Let me guess. The repairs are easy, cheap, and identical, so you should have them fixed in a day or two, right? And I bet you'll be swamped with customers as there's nothing like a murder to get people coming to check out the scene in their droves. It'll be great for business. Murder Island is what they'll call it. Ah, I see you already have a sign made." I indicated the white board with fresh paint, offering rowing boat rentals to Murder Island for a vastly inflated price I knew he'd have no trouble getting.

"A man's gotta make a living," he muttered, eyes lowering.

"Sure, and I'm not judging. I suppose you know what happened out there?"

"Course I do. I know most of the cops and had a word with that couple, Babs and Bob, who were very chatty. I think they might have been drunk, but they filled me in on most of it. Nasty business."

"It sure was, but we made it out alive."

"You figured it all out, didn't you? I knew you would." John's hand slapped over his mouth as he turned away to hide his expression, but I already knew that he'd recognised me somehow.

"When did you figure out who I was?"

"The moment you arrived."

"But you hadn't called in the murder to the police? Surely you should have?"

"Max, I think I better explain things. It's not what you think."

"Then explain. I hate loose ends, and you're the last, so let's hear it."

John looked into my eyes and said, "I had every faith in you. Look, that bunch of crazies have been causing no end of grief for everyone around here for years. Decades actually. It's like some weird cult on the island, but they never get into any actual trouble that could warrant them being told to leave."

"And it means you have a business renting the boats."

"Yeah, sure. Over the years, there have been a few deaths, some of them suspicious, but nobody could ever prove anything. I went over to the island to do a spot of fishing yesterday and set up in my usual spot. White was down the coast a little, as oblivious as always, and didn't even see me. I cast off, then saw the body of Pink and packed up straight away and headed back here. I knew this was my chance to get the cops involved right away and hopefully get the killer caught."

"You knew it was murder?"

"It was obvious, wasn't it? The line around his throat couldn't be an accident. Anyway, I scarpered, but not a minute after I arrived back here you came looking for a rental, and I recognised you. The sad truth is that the police around here have been called out to the island multiple times for deaths, but never found the killer, so when I saw you I couldn't believe my luck. Finally, someone who was actually good at catching criminals. I did a quick check of your wiki page after I rented you the boat and knew you were the man for the job."

"So you didn't call the police?"

"No, and I'm sorry, but I knew if anyone could figure it out, you could."

"So it was you who nobbled the boats?"

John hung his head and mumbled, "Yes. I thought it would force you to stay there and solve the crime. Turns out, maybe the other deaths were accidents, as the last thing I expected was for it to be a lady with a grudge."

"I'd call it more than a grudge, but go on."

"That's about it, really. I recognised you from something I saw online about you being a great amateur detective, and how everyone loves Anxious, so rather than call the cops I decided to ensure you stayed there to solve the case."

"You put me and everyone else at enormous risk. We nearly drowned when we got in the boat, and another person had been murdered."

"But I didn't know about the other murder, and I thought I'd rigged the boats to spring leaks before anyone actually got in them. It was easy enough to do, but I must have been too cautious, so they only sank once they had extra weight. Maybe I should have stuck with taking the oars, but I thought you might be able to rig something up and get away."

"That's nuts! You saw a corpse and rather than alert the authorities you left me to solve the murder?" I was suddenly overcome with a deep lethargy and had to sit on the edge of the workbench and grip the sides for fear of toppling over.

"You okay? You need anything? How about a cuppa?"

"I've already had two coffees, but yes, another would be good. I've been up all night and seen things I never thought I'd see in my life, but I think more than anything it was the water."

"What about the water?"

"Can I have that coffee first?"

"Sure, mate. Hang in there." Looking genuinely concerned, John rushed off to his workshop and I waited, trying to stay awake, focusing on the cry of the gulls as I stared at the dark blot out to sea that now finally had a name. Murder Island. It was certainly apt, but I wondered if Trippy Island might have been more appropriate. What would happen now? Would the water be shut off? Would the residents leave? It didn't matter. It wasn't my concern. The main thing was, I'd solved the murder, even if it did mean getting marooned by a very peculiar boat renter.

John returned with two coffees and handed me one, which I sipped gratefully, my dry lips stinging; I made a mental note to get some new lip balm.

"You don't know about the water? It's what I thought this was all about. They have these strange rituals with the water they get from an old well, although I have no idea how that works with them being out at sea. It's got something in it that makes you go funny in the head, and I nearly died when I drank too much of it. That's why they stay there. They can't get enough of it, and it makes them more and more strange the longer they drink it. You've never heard anything about it?"

"Absolutely nothing, although it explains a lot now. That's probably why a few of them have died over the years and seemed to croak it in one weird way or another eventually. It's been going on since way before my time, and there are loads of stories floating about. Makes sense. They drink this weird water, get trippy, and do something dumb or overdose like you did. What was it like?"

"Kinda nice, as long as it was just a little. But too much and it was horrendous and knocked me unconscious. Don't go near it. Although, I imagine it will get sealed off anyway."

"Shame. I wouldn't mind trying some," he chuckled. "You hear stories from the old-timers around here about there being secret wells, or they reckon when they were kids they'd drink water from certain streams then have visions. I always thought it was bunk, but maybe there was something to it after all."

"I think they were probably telling the truth. Maybe it's all around this area, and some time in the past someone found the fresh water source out there in the cave so installed the pump, and ever since it's been a very well-kept secret."

"How cool is that?" he gushed, eyes wide.

"Either very cool, or very dumb. It's lethal. I told the detectives and have to go and give a proper statement as soon as I have the energy, but at least the killer was caught."

"Max, I'm so sorry I did this to you. I was so sick of people dying and nothing being done, so I wanted you to solve this one. I know I put you and the others in so much danger, but I promise I was going to come and check on you this morning, but you beat me to it thanks to your wife."

"Ex-wife," I corrected. "If she hadn't sent for the coastguard who knows how long we'd have been out there."

"I swear I was coming for you this morning."

"And what if we'd been dead?"

"Um, yeah, well, that would have been a real downer."

For a moment we said nothing, then I almost choked on my coffee as I laughed. John chuckled as he shook his head.

"It would have been a real downer indeed," I agreed once I'd recovered.

"Forgive me?"

"I do, but you'll have to tell the police the truth. I'm going later today, but I want you to promise that you'll go straight away and clear things up. It's the right thing to do."

John nodded. "You may not believe this, but I am an honourable man. I'll get right on it. And thank you. You solved the crime, and I bet you any money that if you hadn't been stranded there the police would have never figured it out."

"That's something we'll never know, isn't it?" I drained my mug, nodded my thanks, then with Anxious skipping about my legs, we hurried back to Min and Vee where I collapsed into the chair and slept for several hours before I was awoken by a delightful smell.

Life was back to normal, or as normal as it could ever be, and as I ate a bacon sandwich outside Vee with Min and Anxious by my side, I knew it was going to be a beautiful day.

The End

Except it isn't. Read on for the recipe that Max used to cook an incredible one-pot wonder. It's simple but delicious, and a guaranteed winner with friends and strangers alike. Just don't drink the water if they offer you any!

The next book in the series is a rather frosty affair as Max spends his first Christmas in his classic campervan. What can we expect? Snow, food, plenty of vanlife struggles in the depths of winter, and there may even be a murder mystery to solve.

Yes. I guarantee it!

First, let's cook.

Recipe

Simple Sea Bass Stew

This is a really speedy one-pot wonder, so great if you and the gang are stuck on an island, with no sign of a Deliveroo option. Don't let the simplicity fool you though. It's beyond tasty, and pretty much foolproof, and really does the fish the justice it deserves.

Ingredients

- Olive oil - a few tablespoons
- Onion - 1 chopped
- Garlic - 2 cloves crushed
- Carrots - 2 sliced into coins
- Fennel seeds - 1 tsp
- White wine - 150ml
- Chopped tomatoes - 1 tin, with their juice
- Stock - 250ml light vegetable or chicken stock
- Thyme - 1 tsp
- Ground almonds - 2 tbsp
- Crushed chilli flakes - 1 tsp
- Salt and freshly ground black pepper to taste
- Sea bass - 4 fillets skinned and chopped into 1" pieces

Method

Use any firm white fish, get creative and add prawns, mussels, or other shellfish.

- Heat the oil in a wide pot and gently sauté the onion, garlic, carrot, and fennel seeds until glistening and the onions are just starting to colour.
- Add the white wine and let it bubble away for ten minutes or so to reduce. Scrape up any tasty caramelised bits from the bottom of the pan.
- Add the tinned tomatoes, stock, thyme, ground almonds, and chilli flakes. Give it a good stir and cook it down on a low heat for 20-30 minutes until thickened a little and the veg is all cooked through. Season to taste.
- Gently lower in the fish and let it blip away for 5 minutes or so.
- Turn the heat off, cover with a lid, and allow the residual heat to cook the fish through (another 2-3 mins).
- Done, *buen provecho!*

Good crusty bread, and a green salad should stave off hunger until the rescuers arrive. Bulb fennel, potatoes, and sweet peppers would all make great additions to make this a more robust affair. If baking your own bread is too time-consuming, try flatbreads like Max did. There are a plethora of recipes, all of which take no longer than ten minutes including prep time.

From the Author

The next book will be full of Christmas magic and perhaps a murder mystery to keep you intrigued and guessing. All in good fun, and lighthearted, with nothing too gruesome, but enough suspects and misadventure to keep you up late at night to find out whodunit and why.

Christmas Corpse will be book 11 in the series, and then there will be four more, so the complete series will be 15 books long. That should see us through to a grand finale where we finally learn what the future will hold for Max, Min, and Anxious. I for one can't wait to discover what that might be, but in the meantime we still have quite a few adventures to go on together so please grab a copy of Christmas Corpse and settle under a blanket to enjoy the latest murder mystery.

Be sure to stay updated about new releases and fan sales. You'll hear about them first. No spam, just book updates at www.authortylerrhodes.com.

You can also follow me on Amazon www.amazon.com/stores/author/B0BN6T2VQ5.

Connect with me on Facebook www.facebook.com/authortylerrhodes/

Printed in Great Britain
by Amazon